SONGS

FOR THE

FLAMES

ALSO BY JUAN GABRIEL VÁSQUEZ

The Informers

The Secret History of Costaguana

The Sound of Things Falling

Lovers on All Saints' Day

Reputations

The Shape of the Ruins

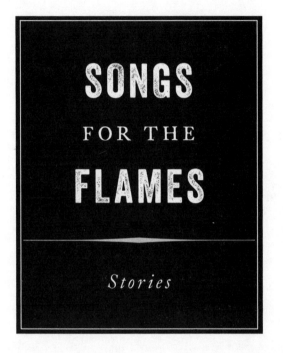

SONGS

FOR THE

FLAMES

Stories

JUAN GABRIEL VÁSQUEZ

Translated from the Spanish by Anne McLean

RIVERHEAD BOOKS • NEW YORK • 2021

RIVERHEAD BOOKS
An imprint of Penguin Random House LLC
penguinrandomhouse.com

English translation copyright © 2020 by Anne McLean
Copyright © 2018 by Juan Gabriel Vásquez

First published in Colombia as *Canciones para el incendio* by
Penguin Random House Grupo Editorial, S. A. S., Bogotá, in 2018.

First published in Great Britain as *Songs for the Flames* by MacLehose Press, an imprint of
Quercus Publishing Ltd., a division of Hachette UK Limited, London, in 2020.

First North American edition published by Riverhead, 2021.

Image on page 237 courtesy of the author.

Library of Congress Cataloging-in-Publication Data

Names: Vásquez, Juan Gabriel, 1973– author. | McLean, Anne, 1962– translator.
Title: Songs for the flames : stories / Juan Gabriel Vásquez;
translated from the Spanish by Anne McLean.
Other titles: Canciones para el incendio. English.
Description: New York : Riverhead Books, 2021. | First published in the Spanish language as
Canciones para el incendio by Juan Gabriel Vásquez by Penguin Random House Grupo Editorial,
S. A. U., in 2019. First published in English by MacLehose Press in 2020.
Identifiers: LCCN 2020037566 (print) | LCCN 2020037567 (ebook) |
ISBN 9780593190135 (hardcover) | ISBN 9780593190159 (ebook)
Subjects: LCSH: Vásquez, Juan Gabriel, 1973– —Translations into English. |
LCGFT: Short stories.
Classification: LCC PQ8180.32.A797 C3613 2021 (print) |
LCC PQ8180.32.A797 (ebook) | DDC 863/.64—dc23
LC record available at https://lccn.loc.gov/2020037566
LC ebook record available at https://lccn.loc.gov/2020037567

Printed in the United States of America
1st Printing

BOOK DESIGN BY LUCIA BERNARD

For Carlota and Martina,
companions on the journey

They assaulted him interminably
the sacred and trivial memories
that are our destiny,
those mortal memories as vast as a continent.

—JORGE LUIS BORGES, "THE END"

I want to know who my past belongs to.

—JORGE LUIS BORGES, "ALL OUR YESTERDAYS"

CONTENTS

SONGS

FOR THE

FLAMES

WOMAN ON THE RIVERBANK

I

I have always wanted to write the story the photographer told me, but I could not have done so without her permission or her collusion: other people's stories are inviolable territory, or that's how it's always seemed to me, because often there is something in them that informs or defines a life, and stealing them in order to write them is much worse than revealing a secret. Now, for reasons that don't matter, she has allowed me this usurpation, and in return has only asked that I tell the story just as she told it to me that night: without tweaks, embellishments, or pyrotechnics, but also without muting anything. "Begin where I begin," she said. "Begin with my arrival at the ranch, when I saw the woman." And that's what I intend to do here, and I'll do so fully aware that I am the way she has found to see her story told by someone else and thus to understand, or try to understand, something that has always escaped her.

————

The photographer had a long name and two long surnames, but everyone always called her Jay. She had become something of a legend over the years, one of those people others knew things about: that she always dressed in black, that she wouldn't have a sip of aguardiente even to save her life. Everyone knew she talked unhurriedly with people before taking her camera out of her bag, and more than once journalists wrote their articles based on material she remembered, rather than what they had managed to find out; it was known that other photographers followed her or spied on her, thinking she didn't notice, and tended to stand behind her in a futile attempt to see what she saw. She had photographed Colombian violence more assidu-ously (and also with more empathy) than any other photojour-nalist, and the most heartrending images of our war were hers: the one of an old lady weeping in the roofless ruins of a church that guerrillas had blown up with a gas cylinder; the one of a young woman's arm with the initials, carved with a knife and already scarring, of the paramilitary group that had murdered her son in front of her. Now things were different in certain for-tunate places: violence was retreating and people were getting to know something like tranquility again. Jay liked visiting those places when she could, to relax, to escape her routine, or simply to witness firsthand those transformations that would once have seemed illusory.

That's how she reached Las Palmas. The ranch was what was left of the ninety thousand hectares that had once belonged to her hosts. The Galáns had never left the province of Los Llanos, nor did they have plans to renovate the old house, and they lived there contentedly, walking barefoot on the dirt floor without startling the hens. Jay knew them because she'd visited the same house twenty years before. Back then the Galáns had rented her the room of one of their daughters, who had gone to study agronomy in Bogotá, and from the window Jay could see the mirror of water, which was what they called a river some hundred meters wide and so calm it looked like a lagoon; the capybaras swam across the river without being pushed off course by the current, and in the middle of the water sometimes a bored black caiman surfaced, floating perfectly still.

Now, on this second visit, Jay would not sleep in that room full of someone else's things, but in the comfortable neutrality of a guest room with two beds and a nightstand between them. (She would use only one bed, and even had a hard time deciding which one.) Everything else was the same as before: there were the capybaras and the caimans, and the calm water, the stillness of which had been increased by the drought. Most of all, there were the people: because the Galáns, maybe due to their reluctance to leave the ranch except to buy supplies, had managed to get the world to come to them. Their table, an enormous wooden board next to a coal-burning stove, was invariably full of people from all over, visitors from the neighboring ranches or from Yopal, friends of their daughters with or without them, zoologists or veterinarians or cattle ranchers who came to talk about their problems. That's how it was this time too. People drove two or three hours to come and see the Galáns; Jay had driven seven, and she'd done so with pleasure, taking time to rest when she stopped for gas, opening the windows of her old jeep to enjoy the changing smells along the road. Some places have a certain magnetism, perhaps unjustified (that is, made up of our mythologies and our superstitions). For Jay, Las Palmas was one of those places. And that's what she was looking for: a few days of quiet among spoonbills and iguanas that climbed down from the trees to eat fallen mangoes, in a place that in other times had been a territory of violence.

So the night she arrived, there she was, sitting under a tube of white light, eating meat and chunks of fried green plantain with a dozen strangers who were obviously strangers to one another as well. They were talking about whatever—how the region had been pacified, how there was no longer extortion, and how cattle were rarely stolen anymore—when she heard the greeting of a woman who had just arrived.

"Buenas y santas," she said.

Jay looked up to say hello, as everyone did, and heard her apologize without looking at anyone, and saw her pull up a plastic chair, and felt something akin to recognition. It took a few seconds to remember or discover that she'd met her right there, at Las Palmas, twenty years earlier. She, however, did not remember Jay.

Later, when the conversation had moved over to the hammocks and rocking chairs, Jay thought: Better this way.

Better that she hadn't recognized her.

II

Twenty years earlier, Yolanda (that was the woman's name) had arrived as part of a retinue. Jay had noticed her from the start: the self-restraint of a guarded prisoner, the tense steps, that way of moving as if she were in a hurry or carrying out an errand. She wanted to appear more serious than she actually was, and most of all more serious than the men in the group. During breakfast on the first day, when the table was moved to the shade of a tree from which mangoes fell with the dry thud of a bocce ball (and yes, there was the waiting iguana), Jay watched the woman and listened to her speak, and watched the men and listened to them speak, and learned they were coming from Bogotá and that the man with the mustache, to whom the others spoke with meekness and even reverence, was a second-tier politician whose favors the region's landowners sought. They called him Don Gilberto, but in the use of his first name, for some reason, Jay detected more respect than if they'd called him by his surname or his position. Don Gilberto was one of those men who spoke without looking at anyone or using anyone's name, but everyone always knew to whom his words or suggestions or orders were directed. Yolanda had sat beside him with her back straight, as if she were holding a notebook ready to write things down, receive instructions, or take dictation. As she took her place on the bench (outside there were no chairs, just a long bench made of planks of wood that all the diners comically had to pick up at once in order to sit on it), she had moved her plate and cutlery away from the man's: five centimeters, no more, but Jay had noticed the gesture and found it eloquent. In the light that opened between them, in her painstaking wish that they not touch, something was happening.

They talked about the upcoming elections; they talked about saving the country from the communist threat. They talked about a dead body that had floated down the river in recent days, and everyone agreed that he must have done something: things like that don't happen to people with nothing to hide. Jay didn't mention the house she'd visited that morning, a half hour's drive away, where a schoolteacher had been accused of indoctrinating the children, found guilty, and decapitated as a lesson to his adolescent pupils; nor did she mention the photographs she'd taken of the pupil whose fate it had been to find the head on his teacher's desk. She did talk, however, of the music of the plains: one of the men at the table turned out to have written several songs; Jay had heard one of them, and surprised the rest (and surprised herself) by reciting the chorus, some lines with galloping riders and an evening sun the color of a pair of lips. She felt she had called attention to herself, perhaps improperly. She also felt that she'd eased things for Yolanda; that the men's gazes on Yolanda became lighter. She felt her wordless gratitude.

Before the last cup of coffee, Señor Galán said: "This afternoon there are horses for anyone who wants to ride. Mauricio will show you around and you can see the property."

"And what is there to see?" asked the politician.

"Oh," Galán said, "you can see everything here."

Jay let the hours slip by in a green hammock, alternating between beer and sugary *aguapanela*, taking catnaps and reading a book by Germán Castro Caycedo. At the agreed time, she approached the stables. There they were: four saddled horses looking at the same point on the horizon. The man who was going to guide them was wearing rolled-up trousers and a knife on his belt; Jay noticed the skin of his bare feet, cracked and split like desiccated earth, like a dried-up riverbed. The man was tightening girths and lengthening reins as the guests mounted their horses, but he never looked anyone in the face, or he had the kind of features that gave that impression: hard cheekbones, grooves instead of eyes. He pointed Jay toward a horse, off on its own, that she thought too skinny; once in the saddle, she felt comfortable on the mount and forgot her objections. When they set off, she noticed that the politician had not come. Yolanda and three of her colleagues were there: the one with the pretentious sideburns, the one with the slicked-back hair, and the one with the lisp who spoke loudly (and rather aggressively) to cover it up or attenuate his hang-ups.

The sky had cleared: a yellow light shone in their faces as they advanced across arid land, past skulls of cows and capybaras, beneath the flight of attentive vultures. The heat had eased off, but there was no wind, and Jay felt sweat on her lower back. Every once in a while she caught a vague whiff of something decomposing. There was a wool blanket on top of Jay's saddle, to soften the rigors of the hard leather, but she must have been doing something wrong, since twice she had tried to gallop and twice she'd felt pain in her pelvis. So she stayed at the back, as if she were looking after the group. Up ahead, Mauricio pointed things out wordlessly, or speaking so quietly that Jay didn't manage to hear. It didn't matter: she just had to look in the direction of his arm to see the unusually colored bird, the huge wasps' nest, the armadillo that caused a stir in the group.

At a certain moment, Mauricio stopped. He gestured for silence and pointed toward a cluster of trees that Jay wouldn't have called a forest. At the heart of the little wood, its head raised as if sniffing the air, was a deer.

"How lovely," Yolanda whispered.

That was the last thing Jay heard her say before the accident. The horses and their riders set off again, and what happened next happened very quickly. Jay didn't notice everything, the sequence of things at the moment they happened, but explanations abounded later: that Yolanda had let go of the reins, that her horse had started to gallop, that Yolanda had squeezed her legs (the reflex of someone trying to keep her balance) and the horse had bolted. This Jay did see: the horse whirled around and took off at an explosive speed toward the ranch, and Yolanda could do nothing but hold on to its neck (she didn't even try to grab the reins, or she reached for them and couldn't find them in the midst of her efforts not to fall off), and that was when Mauricio also took off in a miraculous maneuver, something Jay had never seen before, and cut off the rebel horse's route with his horse, and with his horse's body and his own body crashed into it and toppled it. It was an unbelievably dexterous movement, and would have turned Mauricio briefly into a hero (the one who nips a dangerous situation in the bud and prevents it getting out of hand) if Yolanda had not been thrown forward in a bad way, if her head had not smashed against the ground, against the dry cracks from which dust-covered stones jutted out.

Jay dismounted from her horse to help (a dancer's leap), though there was nothing she could have done. Mauricio, however, was already taking a radiotelephone out of a saddlebag and calling the people at the ranch to tell them to send a car, to start looking for a doctor. The fallen horse was back on its feet now. It stood there quietly, looking nowhere in particular: it had forgotten its urgency to return home. Yolanda was also quiet, lying facedown, with her eyes closed and her arms under her body, like a little girl sleeping on a cold night.

Later, when Señor Galán took Yolanda to a hospital in the city, there was much debate over the actions of the plainsman. He should not have knocked over the other horse, some said; others argued that he'd done the right thing because a horse that bolts is more dangerous for its rider the farther it's allowed to run (the speed, the difficulty of keeping one's balance). They told anecdotes from other times; they talked about invalid children; they said that growing up on the plains a person *learned how to fall*. Don Gilberto listened to the discussions in silence, with his expression deformed by something that looked less like worry than rage, the anger of the owner of a toy that others have not taken care of. Or maybe Jay was not interpreting correctly. His silence was difficult to read; but during the night, when Galán called from the clinic with the latest news, he looked alarmed. He had begun to drink whiskey from the same glass in which he'd been served *aguapanela*, lying in a colorful hammock, but not rocking, rather anchored to the tile floor by a foot with dirty toenails. His whole being was a question. The information he'd received did not satisfy him.

Yolanda was in an induced coma. Her left arm was badly bruised, but nothing was broken; her head, though, had received a blow that could have killed her instantly, and which had provoked a hematoma with unpredictable consequences. The doctors had already trepanned her skull to relieve the pressure of the blood, but there was still a risk, or, to be more accurate, it was not yet possible to name all the many risks that might remain. "We're not through to the other side," said the man who'd spoken to Galán, perhaps using the same words the doctor had used to tell him. It was one of the members of the retinue, one of the most obsequious and, at the same time, of the least visible, and it was strange to hear him describe the skin broken by the hard earth, the face swollen and darkened. Don Gilberto received the words with a surly grimace and poured himself more whiskey, and Jay thought of the strange form power can take: it is a subordinate—an assistant, an employee—who apprises us of someone else's fate, someone who matters to us. Maybe that's what made Jay feel, before the man's preoccupation, something cold, something distant.

After midnight, now drunk, or talking as if he was drunk, Don Gilberto said good night. Jay stayed up a while longer, a while made of dense silences or prudent whispers, as if the convalescent were in the next room. The man who lisped had also had quite a few drinks and was now trying to get Jay to accept a too-full glass of whiskey. As she pretended to drink it, Jay felt suddenly invisible, for the rest had begun to speak as if she were not there.

"The boss is scared," one said.

"Of course," said another. "She's not just anyone."

"It's Yolanda, and he . . ."

"Yes. It's Yolanda."

"He'll die if something happens to her."

"He will. If something happens to her, he'll die."

The voices blended together. One voice was all the voices. Jay began to feel weary (that treacherous weariness with which other people's emotions wear us down). She sank into her hammock, and it was as if someone were tucking her in. She didn't know when she fell asleep.

When she woke up, the rest had all gone to their rooms. They'd turned out the light in the walkway where the hammocks hung, so Jay found herself in a dark place of barely perceptible silhouettes. It smelled of burned oil; the only sound, which filled the night, was the chorus of nameless insects and frogs. A light bulb shining in the distance enabled her to reach the open kitchen, walking with difficulty among sleeping dogs and potted geraniums, and find the fridge: she would pour herself a glass of iced sugar water and go to her room, like everyone else. And the next day she'd ask for news of the other woman, spend the morning around the ranch and take a few photos, and after lunch she'd go back to Bogotá. That's what she decided. But then, as she poured herself a glass of *aguapanela* at the big wooden table, her gaze sought the quiet river, maybe to see if the caimans came out at night. She didn't see any caimans, but she did see a silhouette the size of a large capybara sitting upright on the riverbank. Jay walked as far as the wooden fence and from there her eyes, adjusting to the darkness, made out a hat, then a seated man, then that the man was Don Gilberto. Later she would wonder why, instead of going to bed, she had decided to approach the man. Because of what she'd seen at breakfast, perhaps, or perhaps due to the boss's singular preoccupation?

"Good evening," she said when she was near him.

Don Gilberto barely turned. "How are you, señorita?" he said without any interest.

Jay knew that he had carried on drinking and fleetingly wondered if it was wise to stay near him. But her nebulous curiosity was stronger than those precautions. The man was sitting in the dirt—on the sparse grass that grew unconvincingly on the bank—his arms around his knees and back hunched over. Jay looked for a space free of capybara shit and sat down without asking if he minded, not beside the man, but close enough to carry on a conversation. At night, the waters reflected the misty moon, and Jay tried to remember the name of the trail of light the moon makes on the sea. But she couldn't remember, and besides, this wasn't the sea, but a quiet river in the Eastern Plains, and there was no trail here, rather a slight whitish glow.

Jay held out her hand and said her name.

"Yes, I know who you are," Don Gilberto said, forcing his consonants, which came out slurred in any case. "The photographer, no? From Bogotá."

"What a memory," Jay said. "But politicians are like that, you remember everyone."

Don Gilberto did not respond to the comment. Jay added: "I'm so sorry about your assistant."

"Yes," Don Gilberto said. "What do you make of this little problem?"

Little problem? Yolanda could emerge from the coma with serious mental impairment, or with her motor functions damaged; or she might not emerge from it, remain wrapped in that artificial sleep and not come back to life. That was much more than a little problem, Jay thought, and thought her curiosity had not been mistaken.

"Well, I wouldn't call it that," Jay said. "It's a serious matter. Aren't you concerned—?"

"I know it's a serious matter." Don Gilberto cut her off.

"Of course," Jay said. "I didn't—"

"Don't be preaching to me, you don't know her," the man said. "I do. I know who she is and what would happen . . ."

He didn't finish his sentence. "Sorry," Jay said. "That came out wrong."

"If she dies, she dies on me, not on you."

"Yes," Jay said. "Sorry."

Then the man took an aluminum canteen from between his legs, took off the lid that served as a cup, and drank a shot. The aluminum cast a timid flash of white light, like the quiet water. Then Don Gilberto filled the cup again and offered it to Jay.

"No, thank you," she said. She thought that accepting a drink might send the wrong signal.

The man drank the shot and put the lid back on the canteen. "What do you think will happen?" he asked.

"To her?" Jay said stupidly. "I don't know. I'm not a doctor. They say in cases like this there can be aftereffects."

"Yes, but what kind of aftereffects? Do people get left as invalids, for example?"

"I don't know," Jay said. "I imagine that it's possible."

"Or are they left not right in the head? Confused, say, or with amnesia? Do they forget things?"

"Oh, I see," Jay said. "You're worried about what she knows."

Don Gilberto, for the first time, turned his head (his position didn't allow him to do so easily) and looked at Jay. In spite of the semidarkness, Jay saw in his half-closed eyes that sort of drowsiness of someone who's had too much to drink. No, it wasn't drowsiness: it was like something had gotten in his eyes and was irritating them.

"Like what?" Don Gilberto said. "What do you mean?"

"Nothing, nothing," Jay said. "That she works with you and maybe she has important knowledge, important information. Nothing else."

Don Gilberto turned back to look at the river.

"Important knowledge," he repeated.

"Yes," Jay said. "I suppose."

"Well, yes, señorita, I think you're right," Don Gilberto said. He poured himself another shot of whiskey in the canteen lid, then another, as if struck by a kind of urgency, and continued talking. "But it's that one doesn't know, don't you think, one doesn't know what goes on in the head of a person like that. A person who's had an accident like that. Like Yolanda. My assistant. She's in a coma, she might come out okay or she might not, right now she's in a coma. And what happens in her head? What will she remember when she wakes up? Will she not forget anything? Important information, yes. Information from all these years she's been with me: several now, three or four. In years like these, one finds out many things, my friend. Important knowledge. That might be lost, right? You said it. Sure, that's what's worrying me: that the things she knows will get lost. You think that's possible? That she might wake up and will have forgotten things, just like that? You think that happens?"

"Yes," Jay said. "Sadly."

Don Gilberto made an ambiguous noise in his throat: was

it agreement, resignation? She could hear frogs; Jay could hear something that might or might not have been cicadas. She looked at her watch and discovered, in the dim light, that it was already past two in the morning. The night had cooled down, and there was an uncomfortable note in the conversation with the man, a dissonance or some kind of hostility. Jay's curiosity came up against the limit of her weariness. She stood and spoke down toward his hat:

"Well, we'll see how everything is tomorrow."

The hat nodded: "Yes. We'll see."

Jay began to walk back to the house, back to her room. The next day she'd return to Bogotá. The night was blue and black and refreshed by a soundless breeze. She had to be careful not to step where she shouldn't, and this was frustrating, because Jay would have liked to look up and walk without worrying, take deep breaths and smell the dense odors of the ranch. She took a detour so as not to arrive too soon at her bedroom, to hold on to the darkness of the world, and the detour took her to a corner where a single hammock hung. It wasn't a social area: more like a private space where (Jay imagined) Señor Galán would take his siestas. She lay down in the hammock and stayed there, swaying in the darkness, and in the darkness she thought over the day's events: breakfast, the cutlery that Yolanda moved away from her boss's, the ride that started off so well, and then Yolanda's mistake (dropping the horse's reins) and the plainsman's maneuver, that swift and expert maneuver, which in her memory stretched out to allow her to see Yolanda's face, the expression of anxious gravity that transforms our features in an emergency, in a moment of terror, in a second that is the threshold of something serious. And in her memory Don Gilberto's face also appeared, even though he hadn't been there. Jay had jumped down off her horse to help the fallen woman, and there was her boss first, crouched down beside her, stretching out his hand as if he wanted to hold her head, but without actually doing so. When it wants our attention, memory tends to resort to distortion or deceit.

"Shit," Jay said.

A long time later, talking about that day, Jay would leave a gap at this point in the tale. She would explain it by saying that there, in the hammock, she realized something, but she didn't know or never would know what she'd realized. "Shit," she'd said quietly, and she said it the way we say it when we drop a glass and it shatters on the floor, or when we remember something important we've forgotten at home (and we smack ourselves on the forehead, or slam the edge of our fist against the steering wheel). She would tell about standing up from the hammock and beginning to walk to her room, but halfway there (as she was passing the corridor where she'd fallen asleep in a hammock hours earlier) she turned and stepped down onto the ground of the garden, what the Galáns called the garden, and kicked a fallen mango and slipped between the rails of the wooden fence to go down to the riverbank, to the space where the riverbank began, and confirmed that Don Gilberto was still there, sitting beside the quiet water.

Jay arrived spectrally by Don Gilberto and tried to make her presence known by dragging her feet as she got near. She didn't sit beside the man, but almost in front of him, in order to see his face better. And then she said:

"Don Gilberto, I'm so sorry. I just found out."

"What happened?"

Jay thought silence advisable. Don Gilberto spoke again.

"What happened? Did Yolanda die?"

"I'm so sorry," Jay said.

And then she saw it. Jay saw what happened on Don Gilberto's face, an encounter of emotions, a movement of muscles, and later she would think of the miracle of the human face, which could transmit more emotions than we'd learned to name with so few tools. The one Jay saw, the one that manifested itself in the slanted eyes and the arch of his brows, was relief. It is not impossible that there might have been sadness there first, or consternation, or a fleeting depression, but the depression or consternation or sadness gave way to relief, and the impression was so strong that Jay, who had come to the riverbank looking for that revelation, had to look away, as if ashamed of what she saw.

———

Shortly before first light, something woke her. A rooster crowed in the distance, maybe on another farm. Jay reached for her watch on the bedside table: she hadn't been asleep for three hours yet. She felt a draft and noticed then, with her eyes half shut, that the door to her room was open. But she remembered (or thought she remembered) closing it carefully. A dog must have pushed it, she thought, or the wind. She closed it quietly so she wouldn't wake anyone, and was on her way back to bed when she saw the man.

Don Gilberto was sitting on a plastic chair, his hands on his knees. Jay heard his breathing first and then his words: "Did I frighten you, señorita?"

Jay checked her clothing—full-length pajamas with trousers and shirt—and looked toward the window, toward the door.

"What a shame to frighten you," Don Gilberto said. Now Jay heard in his voice the drunken consonants. "I wanted to tell you about a snag."

"Couldn't you tell me later?" Jay began. "I'm tired, and—"

"No, it has to be now." The man cut her off. "It's that I found something out."

Jay was still standing, a step from the door. She tried to project her voice.

"What?"

"That Yolanda hasn't died," Don Gilberto said. "Incredible, isn't it?"

"Ah, yes. I was told."

"You were told? How strange, eh? Who told you?"

Jay didn't answer. The rooster, in the distance, crowed again. She could not see Don Gilberto's face clearly; absurdly, Jay thought of a Francis Bacon painting. Against the white wall, Don Gilberto's sloping shoulders gave him a melancholy appearance, as if the lie had saddened him, but in his voice (in the alcohol in his voice) there was a willingness to threaten, to cause fear.

"If you knew how little I liked—" he said.

"Look, Don Gilberto, I don't know what you've been told, but I—"

"—being deceived. How little I like being deceived. That's really nasty, girl."

Girl, Jay noticed.

"I was told," she said.

"No, I don't believe you were. Nobody told you anything. And what a drag, no? What a little problem. What a bitch of a problem we've got."

"It was a mistake," Jay said.

"You're fucking right it was a mistake," the man said. "You just don't do that kind of thing, honey. Is it going to be up to me to teach you a lesson? Teach you not to do that sort of thing?"

Jay realized she was standing between the man and the door. She moved toward the window to make herself visible, because the first workers would soon be going out, and also because that left the way free for the man: like when you open the door and turn on the outside light to lure a moth out of your room.

The man said: "You people just never learn." And then: "You're leaving today, aren't you, girl?" And then: "Yes, you're leaving today. So I won't have to run into you again. What a drag."

He stood up slowly, as if it was hard work carrying the weight of his own shoulders, and walked out into the early morning.

III

"And have you been to Las Palmas before?"

Twenty years later, Jay found herself again facing that woman whose death she had feigned. All day Saturday, crossing paths with her in the walkways and sitting at the same table for breakfast and lunch, she had tried to see in her features some vestige of what had happened. Would that not be carved into her face? Could someone go through an experience like that without her face registering it forever? But what there was in Yolanda's features (Jay now realized she'd never known her surname) gave nothing away. She must have been approaching fifty, Jay estimated, but there was something infantile in her gaze, something innocent. And now this innocent woman was asking Jay if she had come to Las Palmas before. And Jay didn't even hesitate.

"Never," she said. "This is my first time."

"And do you like the plains?"

"Yes, very much. It's like another world."

If Yolanda wanted to play the cliché game, Jay could give as good as she got. They were on the veranda where the hammocks were, each with a beer in hand, waiting for the cook to tell them dinner was ready. Jay had not sought out this situation, but had planned on sitting beside Yolanda at dinner. It hadn't been necessary: she found her here, putting insect repellent on her ankles and arms, and asked her for a little; and that's how they began talking, at first with the fading evening light, then under the white light of a neon tube.

"I come every year," Yolanda said. "Of course, it's easy for me, because I live in Yopal. You're from Bogotá, aren't you?"

"I am."

"Oh, I could never live there. It's so cold."

"Well, I travel a lot. That helps."

"For your work, no? You're a photographer."

"Exactly."

"And what kind of photos do you take?"

"Journalism," Jay said. "I spent many years photographing the conflict."

"The conflict?"

"The violence, the war. So I've been all over the country, from one side to the other."

"Of course," Yolanda said. "And what were you looking for? The sites?"

"The sites, yes, but the people as well. The victims of the war, so many of them." Pause. "But, how strange, I never came to this part of the plains." Pause. "Nearby, but never over here." Pause. "There was a lot of violence around here, wasn't there?"

"Yes, at one time. Not anymore."

"And nothing happened to you? Or your family?"

"Things are much better now," Yolanda said.

"Everywhere," Jay said. "You can't imagine what it's like, traveling to places I went ten or twenty years ago for a massacre or whatever, and seeing that it's so different today. People's faces change when they're not afraid. People's faces say so much."

"And they don't mind you taking their photos?"

From the kitchen, an open patio where a skinny black woman moved like she was a whole team, came cooking smells and the sounds of pots and pans. They were going to eat a chicken that the Galáns had instructed should be killed that afternoon. Jay had gone to see the spectacle of the plucking; she hadn't wanted to keep watching when the cook held the hen down on a board by its neck, and took out a knife.

"No," Jay answered. "Well, sometimes. But almost never, because first we've talked, we've gotten to know each other. I can't stand it when some photographers go around hunting other people's sadness. I've never taken a photo of anyone who hasn't first told me a story." Pause. "You, for example. If I were going to take photos of you, first I'd sit down and talk for a good while, until you told me your stories. What had happened to you. What the war had left you."

Yolanda let out a tiny laugh. "With me you'd be wasting your time. I was fine."

"Sure," Jay said. "But that's strange. Everybody has something to tell." Pause. "I've never been in this part of the plains, as I said, but I have been near here. In Arauca, near the Venezuelan border. There was a lot of trouble there twenty years ago."

"Was there? I don't remember."

"I knew a woman back then. She'd lived through the worst years without anything happening to her. When the bodies of murdered people floated down the river, she'd see them and sometimes recognize them, but nothing ever happened to her or her family. Later she began to work for a politician, and after two, three years, she came to trust him. They traveled together on his campaigns. She became his right hand, and he said to her all the time: 'What would I do without you? I'd die without you.' That sort of thing. One day, in a hotel in Bogotá, the boss knocked at her door. She opened the door, of course: what else could she have done? At six in the morning. That's what that woman told me: that it had been at six in the morning. I don't know why it mattered so much."

Yolanda was looking toward the darkness, or toward the river that slipped by in silence beyond the darkness. "I think there's a woman on the riverbank," she said.

Jay didn't say anything.

"A few days ago they found a python nearby. We were sitting here on the patio talking, like you and I are, and one of the workers came and told us. The python was looking for food. They found it on the other side of the river, where the woods are. Can you imagine the fear?"

Jay turned toward the river, but she didn't see anyone. From the other patio, however, came the black woman. "Dinner's ready," she said with a sweet smile. She was missing her two front teeth.

The next day, while she was packing, Jay spent a few minutes cleaning her camera. She had several hours' drive ahead of her; she had to call the police to check the state of the road, if any landslides or accidents had been reported, or if there was no news. But outside it was sunny and the busiest moment had passed, when the workers come to have breakfast with the guests and the smell of their work clothes mixes for a few seconds with the smell of the coffee and the eggs. The house had entered its brief midmorning quiet spell: everyone had gone back to work and the visitors had gone to see animals and the Galáns were sitting down going through invoices or settling up with a supplier or a client. Jay left her room, camera in hand, and looked for Yolanda. She found her taking a siesta in a hammock and, without warning, took a photograph of her.

Yolanda opened her eyes. "What happened?"

"Sorry," Jay said. "You don't mind?"

"But here?"

"Yes," Jay said. "Right there, why not."

Yolanda lay back again. Jay gave her a couple of instructions, moved a can of beer out of the shot, and walked around the hammock to find the best light, the best angle. Yolanda covered her face with her hands; the shutter sounded once, twice. Yolanda asked: "Doesn't it matter if I'm crying?"

"It doesn't matter," Jay said. "Cry as much as you want."

THE DOUBLE

E rnesto Wolf. In the class roll our surnames were next to each other, because there don't tend to be too many names after mine in Colombia (unless it's a foreign one or some curiosity: Walsh or Zapata, Yammara or Zúñiga). The day of the lottery that would or would not send us into the army, alphabetical order meant that I would pick before he did. In the burgundy-colored velvet bag there were only two little balls left, one blue and one red, where a short time before there had been almost fifty, the number of students who were eligible for military service that year. Picking the red ball would send me into the army; the other would send my friend. The system was very simple.

That happened in the Teatro Patria, a building attached to the Cavalry School, where now they show bad movies and where there used to be, once in a while, a comedy, the odd concert, a magic act. A magic act, yes, that's what the lottery was like. All the boys in the last year of high school acted as the audience along with a few more or less supportive teachers. Onstage, three actors: a lieutenant with plasterwork hair (maybe he was a lieutenant, but I'm not sure; I don't really remember his shoulders or his lapel or his breast pocket, and anyway I've never been able to recognize ranks), a female assistant in uniform, and a volunteer who had gone up, unwillingly, to participate in the magic, to pick out the little ball that could deprive him of civilian life for a year. The assistant, smelling of mothballs, held up the bag of lottery balls. I put in my hand, pulled out the blue ball, and before I had time to think that I had condemned my friend, he had invaded the stage to embrace me and provoke the indignation of the officer and the complicity of the assistant, a wink from her blue-shadowed, generously mascaraed eyelid.

The soldier, lieutenant, or whatever he was, took out his Kilometrico ballpoint and signed an ivory-colored, water-marked, and embossed sheet of paper, folded it in three, and handed it to me as if he were handing me a smelly rag, at the same time biting the plastic pen cap: the white, saliva-covered cap, shiny against a background of yellow teeth. Ernesto and the woman, meanwhile, were talking; he didn't want to draw his red ball, since it was the last one and the procedure seemed superfluous to him, and there was no possible surprise for the audience, the mass of high school grads who shared the same idea of the entertainment: that the guy next to him would be recruited. But the woman and maybe her makeup convinced Ernesto to reach his hand in, to take out the ball; and convinced him of other things too. The next day, at lunchtime, my telephone rang.

"What a body she had, bro," Ernesto's groggy voice said to me. "You couldn't tell from the uniform."

We saw each other afterward a couple of times, and then seeing each other didn't depend on us. Unscrupulously anxious, offensively meek, Ernesto Wolf joined the Ayacucho Company of the Tenth Brigade, in Tolemaida, at the end of August that same year. *Ayacucho*: the cacophony meant nothing to him, except a vague echo from primary school. Ernesto, grandson of a foreigner who was once accused of a lack of patriotism in a major newspaper, son of a father who had grown up not quite sure where he was from—although he had been baptized with a name from the calendar of saints, so as not to be out of place—didn't know much about Ayacucho in particular or the wars of independence in general. I thought that friendship obliged me to give him a hand with his patriotism. I got up early one Sunday; I snapped a Polaroid of the Monument to the Heroes and took it to Tolemaida between the pages of the newspaper.

AYACUCHO

PICHINCHA

CARABOBO

Two cacophonies and a disguised insult, all carved into the semiprecious stone of national independence: this I handed to Cadet Wolf. It was August, as I said, and the wind was already getting up, and on the patches of grass around the monument people had set up improvised lines and were selling kites, geometric tissue paper with bamboo frames that could never withstand the onslaught of a single gust of mountain wind. In Tolemaida, which wasn't in the mountains but down in the tropical lowlands, there was no wind; in Tolemaida the air didn't move, didn't seem to ever move. Lance Corporal Jaramillo would drape an old boa constrictor over the cadets' shoulders, and the length of time they had to carry it depended on the extent of their insubordination; Lance Corporal Jaramillo, as threat or dissuasion, told the Company the only urban legend there was in that rural region, about the dungeon of Cuatro Bolas, where an immense black man had his way with rebellious recruits in an unholy manner. For a year, Ernesto Wolf told more stories about Lance Corporal Jaramillo than he'd ever told about anyone. Lance Corporal Jaramillo was responsible for the immobility of the air, for the fevers, for the blisters on their hands from gripping their rifle stocks during firing-range exercises. He was responsible for the tears of the youngest cadets (there were some who were just fifteen, precocious high school graduates) hidden behind the storehouse or in the lavatories, and at night with a smothering pillow over their faces. Lance Corporal Jaramillo. I never knew his first name; I never saw him, but I came to hate him. On Sundays, on visits to the Lancers' School or at the Wolfs' house in Bogotá, Ernesto sat—on the dry grass, if the visit was in Tolemaida; if it was in Bogotá, at the head of the table—and told stories; facing him, his parents and I ate and looked at one another and together we hated Lance Corporal Jaramillo. But now that I think about it, maybe I'm mistaken: Antonio, his father, was present only if the leave day was a Sunday, and he never set foot inside the Lancers' School, just as he'd never entered the Teatro Patria.

One of those Sundays, while we were waiting for the bus that brought Ernesto from Tolemaida when he got leave, stuck in a car with the windows rolled up tight (the dust, the noise of Puente Aranda), Antonio Wolf, who was growing fond of me by then, said out of the blue: "But you wouldn't have wanted." He said it like that, he said that strange, seemingly incomplete phrase, gripping the steering wheel with those hands of an old boxer, of a Bavarian peasant, the hands that would never cease to look like those of a recent arrival, although it hadn't been him but his father who'd been the immigrant. He said it without looking at me, because inside a car people tend not to look at each other. Like a fire or a cinema screen, a car's windshield attracts the gaze, traps and dominates it.

"What?" I said.

"To go like that," he said. "To go and waste time. Ernesto

did want to go. And what for? To learn to swear stupid allegiances and shoot a rifle that he's never going to use again in his life."

I was eighteen years old then. I didn't understand the words: I understood that Antonio Wolf, a man I had come to respect, was talking frankly to me and perhaps also respected me. But I hadn't earned that respect, because it had been chance, not ideas or principles, that had been responsible for my not having to go into that damned place where they learned to swear stupid allegiances and shoot rifles they'd never use again, but where most of all they wasted time, our own time and our parents' time as well, where life got snagged.

And there the Wolfs' life got snagged. Sixteen days before finishing his military service, Ernesto died in the middle of some maneuvers I don't know the name of. A pulley snapped, the rope Ernesto was suspended from fell into the thirty-yard drop between two mountains, Ernesto's body smashed into the rocks at fifty miles per hour, and everyone agreed that he must already have been dead when he fell to the bottom of the valley, where there's a little waterfall the teenagers of the region tend to use as a spot to lose their virginity. I could have gone to the funeral, but I didn't. I made one call, found the Wolfs' telephone line busy, and left it at that. I sent flowers and a note explaining that I was in Barranquilla, which was a lie, of course, and I remember the absurd difficulty I had in deciding between Barranquilla and Cali, which city would seem less unlikely or raise fewer doubts. I didn't find out later if the Wolfs had believed me or if they'd recognized my rude lie: they never answered my note, and I never went to see them after the accident. I began to study law, and halfway through my degree I knew I'd never practice, because I'd written a book of short stories and in the process of doing so I'd realized that I didn't want to do anything else for the rest of my life. I went to Paris. I lived in Paris for almost three years. I went to Belgium. I spent nine months in Belgium, ten minutes from a clandestine village in the Ardennes. In October 1999, I arrived in Barcelona; in December of the same year, while spending the holidays with my family in Bogotá, I met a German woman who had arrived in Colombia in 1936. I asked her questions about her life, about how her family had escaped from the Nazis, about the things she found in Colombia when she arrived; she answered with a freedom that I've never found again and I noted down her answers on the squared pages of a small writing pad, the kind with a picture or a logo running along one edge (in this case it was the phrase *Beware the man of a single book*). Years later I used those pages, those answers— in a word, that life—to write a novel.

The novel was published in July 2004. Its plot turned on a German immigrant who, toward the end of the Second World War, was confined in the Sabaneta, a luxury hotel converted by the Colombian government into a temporary internment camp for enemy citizens (enemies of Roosevelt, sympathizers of Hitler or Mussolini). Researching the novel had been particularly difficult, because some subjects continue to be sensitive or even forbidden in many families of the German community in Bogotá; and that's why it seemed so ironic to me that after it was published so many people came to ask me to listen to *their* story now, that now I should tell *their* story. Months later I was still receiving e-mails from Germans or children of Germans who had read the book and were correcting one or two details—the color of a wall, for example, or the existence of some plant in some precise place—and scolded me for not having done more thorough research and then offered me their stories for my next book. I replied with evasive courtesy (out of superstitions I can't explain, I've never refused any offer outright). And weeks later another similar e-mail would arrive, or a message from someone who knew someone who knew someone who had been in the Hotel Sabaneta and who could give me information if I needed it. And that's why I wasn't surprised to receive, in February 2006, an envelope with a German name on the back. I confess it took me several seconds to recognize it, I confess to having climbed two or three steps of the entrance to my building before the face that belonged to that name appeared in my head. I opened the letter on the stairs, began to read it in the elevator, and finished it standing in the kitchen of my apartment, with my bag still hanging from my shoulder, with the front door wide open and the keys in the lock.

Isn't it strange (the letter said to me), in Spanish there's no word for what I am. If your wife dies you're a widower, if your father dies you're an orphan, but what are you if your son dies? It is so grotesque for your child to die that the language has not learned what to call such people, even though children have been dying before their parents forever and parents have been suffering the deaths of their children forever. I've followed your trail (the letter said to me), but up till now I'd decided not to do anything about it. Not to look for you, not to write, do you know why? Because I hated you. I don't hate you anymore, or rather, there are days when I hate you, I wake up hating you and wishing for your death, and sometimes I wake up wishing your children would die, if you have children. But other days I don't. Forgive me for telling you like this, by letter, one should tell people things like this face-to-face, live and in person, but on this occasion I cannot, because you're over there, of course, you live in Barcelona, and I am here, in a little house in Chía that I bought after the divorce. You know about the divorce, I imagine, because it was the most talked-about one of the year in Bogotá, all the ugly details came to light. Anyway, I'm not going to get into that, what matters now is confessing that I hated you. I hated you because you weren't Ernesto, because but for very little you could have been Ernesto and nevertheless you weren't Ernesto. You went to the same school, knew the same things, played on the same soccer team, were in the same row that day in the Teatro Patria, but you got to the bag of lottery balls first, you got the ball that should have been Ernesto's. You sent him to Tolemaida, and I can't get that out of my head. If you were called Arango or Barrera instead of being called what you are, my son would still be alive, and I would still have my life in my own hands. But my son is dead, he has this fucking surname and he's dead for having this fucking surname, the name that appears on his tombstone. And maybe what's going on is that I can't forgive myself for giving it to him.

But why should I expect you to understand all this? (the letter said to me). When you didn't even have the guts to show up at the cemetery to say goodbye to your lifelong friend. When you live over there, far away from this country where a person does military service and might not come out of it alive, living a comfortable life, what's it going to matter to you? When you've gone into hiding since the death of your friend out of pure fear of showing your face and seeing that there is a destroyed family, that this family could have been yours and wasn't simply by chance. What are you afraid of? Are you afraid it'll be your turn one day? It will (the letter said to me), I swear to you, one day you will face a moment like that, you'll realize that sometimes a person needs others, and if the others aren't around at the right moment, your life can come crashing down. I don't know what would have happened to my life if I could have given you a hug the day of the funeral and said thanks for coming, or if you'd kept coming to the house for a meal once a week like you did when Ernesto was doing his service and had leave. We used to talk about Lance Corporal Jaramillo, Ernesto told us about that dungeon and the snake the cadets had to carry on their shoulders. Sometimes I think I would have endured everything better if I could have remembered those things with you sitting at the table. Ernesto loved you; you were going to be like those friends a person has their whole life. And you could have been a comfort to us, we loved you (the letter said to me), we shared Ernesto's affection for you. But now (the letter said to me) that's all water under the bridge: you weren't there, you hid and denied us your comfort, and things started to go badly at home, until it all came tumbling down. It was at Christmas, already ten years ago, how time flies. I don't really remember what happened, but people told me later that I had chased her around a table, that Pilar had to hide in a bathroom. What I do remember, however, is having taken the car to leave the party, and that I drove without really knowing where I was going, and that only after parking somewhere I realized I was at Puente Aranda, in the same parking lot where the buses from Tolemaida stopped, the same place where you and I used to wait for Ernesto sometimes and where we once had a conversation I'll never forget.

The letter said all this to me. I remember, first of all, having thought: he's sick. He's dying. And I remember the immediate dismay, not sadness or nostalgia or indignation either (although some indignation, provoked by Antonio Wolf's accusations, would have been legitimate). I did not answer the letter; I looked at the back of the envelope, confirmed that the sender's address—that little house in Chía—was complete, and I put the envelope and letter on a bookshelf in my study, between two albums of photos of my daughters, those daughters that Antonio Wolf was threatening. Maybe I chose that place to repudiate the letter, so that the letter would provoke repudiation; and I was successful, without a doubt, because during the year that followed I opened those albums many times and many times I looked at the photos of my daughters, but I never reread the letter. And maybe I would never have reread it if I hadn't received, in January 2007, news of Antonio Wolf's death. One very cold Monday morning I got up, checked my e-mail, and there was a newsletter, sent by the alumni association of my school. His passing—a word I've always despised—was announced, the date and time of the *exequias*—likewise that word—and reminded us that the deceased—one more—was the father of a graduate, but didn't say that his son had died many years before. So three months later, when I had to go back to Bogotá, I stuck the letter in with my papers. I did it because I know myself well, I know my quirks and my manias and knew I'd regret it if I missed the opportunity to see, even if from afar, the house where Antonio Wolf had lived his last years, the years of his decline and death, and where he had written the most hostile and at the same time most intimate letter I'd ever received. I let a few days go by after my arrival, but on the third I took the envelope and, in a borrowed car, drove the twenty miles or so from Bogotá to Chía.

Finding the house was not difficult: Chía is a minuscule town, and walking from one side of it to the other takes no more than fifteen minutes. The numeration of the streets led me to a gated subdivision: ten houses of cheap brick, facing each other in two rows of five and separated by an area paved in the same brick, or bricks the same salmon color that always look new. In the center of the flat space was a soccer ball (a new one: one of those balls with silver and yellow) and a plastic thermos. There were motorcycles parked in front of a few houses; at the end, a shirtless man in sandals disappeared inside the running motor of a Renault 4. And that was as far as I'd gotten, standing on the sidewalk in front of a gatehouse with darkened windows, squinting to see if I could make out the numbers on the houses and guess which one had been Antonio Wolf's, when the guard came out and asked me where I was going. I was more surprised than he was as I watched him return to his cubicle, call through the intercom, and come out again to say: "Go ahead." And ahead I went. Ten, twenty, thirty steps; people looking out of their windows, behind the net curtains, to see the visitor; a door that opens, a woman who comes out. She's about forty. She's wearing a Christmas apron, although Christmas was four months ago, and she's drying her hands; under her arm she's carrying a plastic corrugated folder, the kind that closes and opens with a Velcro strip.

"Here's what Don Antonio left you." The woman handed me the folder. "He told me you were going to come. He also said not to let you in, not even for a glass of water."

There was resentment in her voice, but also obedience: the obedience of someone carrying out an errand they don't understand. I took the folder without looking at her; I wanted to say goodbye, but the woman had already turned around and was walking toward her door.

When I got to the car I put the folder on top of the letter: the two missives with which Antonio Wolf remained present in my life sixteen years after we'd seen each other for the last time. I started the engine, not wanting to stay in front of the house and in front of the guard (a strange sort of embarrassment), but I was already thinking of going into downtown Chía, with its large free parking lot that had no attendants or gates. And that's what I did: I drove down to the shopping district, parked in front of Los Tres Elefantes, and began to look through the contents of the file. None of what I found surprised me. Or rather: before I opened the folder I already knew what I would find, the way you know certain things from deep inside your head, even before you get what we call intuition or a premonition.

The oldest document was a page from the school yearbook. There we are, the two of us, Ernesto and me, in our soccer uniforms, lifting the trophy of a Bogotá tournament. Then there was a copy of the April 1997 issue of the magazine *Cromos*, open at the page that announced, in five short lines, the news of the publication of my first novel. And suddenly I found myself reclining the passenger seat to make more room and organizing all the documents inside the car, using every available surface—the dashboard, the open door of the glove compartment, the back seat, the armrests—to spread out the chronology of my life since Ernesto Wolf's death. There was the news of my books, every review or interview that had appeared in the Colombian press. Some documents were not originals but yellowing photocopies, as if Antonio had found out about the news item too late and had to photocopy the magazine at a library. Others were underlined, not with a pencil, but with cheap ballpoint pens, and in those passages I appeared making grandiloquent or silly declarations, or spouting clichés, or inanely answering a journalist's inane questions. In the articles relating to my novel about Germans in Colombia, there were more underlined passages; and under every one of my comments on exile, life elsewhere, the difficulty of adaptation, memory and the past and the way we inherit the errors of our ancestors, Antonio's lines seemed full of a pride that made me uncomfortable, made me feel dirty, as if it didn't belong to me.

I never managed to find out who the woman who handed me the plastic folder was. At that moment, of course, various options occurred to me, and on my way back to Bogotá I was playing with ideas, imagining Antonio Wolf's unknown life while driving distractedly down the highway. That messenger would be a woman from the village, perhaps a *campesina*; Wolf had hired her as a domestic and then, little by little, he'd come to realize he had no one else in the world. The woman was also on her own and perhaps had a daughter, a young daughter that Wolf would have taken in. I imagined the change in the relationship between two lonely and confused people, imagined scenes of guilty sex that would have scandalized Bogotá society, imagined Wolf saying that this woman would keep living in the house after his death. But most of all I imagined him dedicated to collecting someone else's life, feeling that he was replacing the emptiness that the absence of his son caused in his life with the power of distant documents. I imagined him talking to the woman of that boy who wrote books and lived far away. I imagined him, at night, dreaming that the boy was his son, that his son was living far away and writing books. I imagined him fantasizing of the possibility of lying, of telling that woman that the boy was really his son, and I imagined him feeling, during the brief moments of the lie, the illusion of happiness.

FROGS

After the official speeches—the ambassador, a minister, several generals—after a choir of Korean girls in red berets sang the national anthem, the veterans and their families moved toward the green marquees where they were serving sparkling wine. Now little groups had formed according to the inscrutable inertia of commemorative events, and Salazar found himself surrounded by couples who must have already lost count of the number of drinks they'd had, as the veterans had gone from solemn toasts to the heroes of the Colombia Battalion to reviving their war memories between bursts of loud laughter that shook the glasses in their hands. The sky had clouded over, but nobody seemed worried about an imminent downpour.

And there was Salazar, as he had been so many other years at so many other veterans' reunions. There he was, taking part in the group, standing between two women in tailored suits who didn't even look at him. He saw the men slapping each other on the back and talking about Pork Chop Hill and Old Baldy and telling amusing anecdotes about a time in their lives—weeks, months—that presumably had not been very amusing. The women were talking among themselves, and their lipstick-scented words passed in front of Salazar's face. From the other side of the circle, the tallest man, whom the others called Trujillo, was telling how he'd made the decision to go to Korea: a place he'd never heard of, the location of which he wouldn't have been able to find on a map if his life depended on it, but where he had gone, like four thousand other Colombians, to collaborate in the great international effort to contain the red menace.

"We all wanted to be heroes," Trujillo said, and the rest nodded. "The priest at the school was always telling us the same thing: it doesn't matter where Korea is. Any place is a good place to kill communists." The group exploded in laughter, and then Trujillo looked at Salazar. "And you, sir? Did you volunteer or get recruited?"

"He volunteered," another voice said before Salazar could answer. "This guy was the most eager to go. Even if it meant adding a couple of years to his age so they'd let him."

Salazar was amazed once more at what the years could do to a man's face. The one who'd just spoken was Lieutenant Gutiérrez, who had shared with him the five months of training before deployment. Five months of sleeping on hard camp beds and eating in mess tents so the rank and file could get used to what campaign life would be like, five months lived in anticipation of they didn't know what, five months in which the only information they received about Korea was what appeared in the newspapers, because their superior officers knew as little as they did. Five months outside of life, that life in Bogotá where people were going to see Marlene Dietrich in *Stage Fright* while they, the future soldiers of the Colombia Battalion, were jumping over white walls and dragging themselves across muddy fields always gripping their rifles with both hands; five months of target practice at the Cavalry School's firing range, the crack of the gunshots breaking the cafeteria's windows, and eating from plates shared with the officers because there weren't enough to go around. His plate partner on several occasions, the only officer with whom he'd had any sort of friendship, was Lieutenant Gutiérrez, favored son of a military family whose face, which back then was already hard, had turned over these past fifty years into an eroded landscape: the bald, liver-spotted head, the blue veins at the sad temples, the wrinkles deep as claw marks.

"Oh, you two were together?" Trujillo's wife asked. She was much younger than the rest of them: his second, third marriage?

"Half a century ago," Salazar said. "But not exactly together: I was under the orders of my lieutenant here, wasn't I."

"We were at the Cavalry School, after that we didn't see each other again," Lieutenant Gutiérrez said. "But I could never forget Salazar. He was the one who came with me to look for fugitives."

"Fugitives?"

"In the mornings we didn't take roll call of those who were there, but of those who had snuck off during the night," Lieutenant Gutiérrez said. "Do you remember, Salazar?"

"I remember," Salazar said. And it was true: he did remember, he remembered perfectly. The lieutenant would show up in the barracks at any moment and didn't have to say a word for Salazar to realize: they were going hunting. They looked for the fugitives in the bars, dragged them half naked out of brothels, took them back to the school to nurse their hangovers with sugary *aguapanela*, fully aware that they'd repeat the same routine the next night. One of those days, Major Henríquez—did he remember Major Henríquez?—had taken a risk by having them form up and asking everyone who did not want to go to Korea to take one step forward: a third of the company took that step, and the thunder of boots on pavement took the place of a bad omen. "They're scared shitless, of course, and no wonder," the lieutenant said to Salazar. "They're going to war. And they've only just realized it."

"But we aren't going to fight," Salazar said. "We're going as an occupation force."

"Yeah, is that what they've told you?" the lieutenant said.

"That's what the major says," Salazar said.

"Ah, well, then." The lieutenant smiled. "If that's what the major tells you, I'm sure it's the honest truth."

Yes, I realized too at that moment, Salazar was now thinking. In front of the Pagoda, gusts of wind were making the flags flap and stealing the little choir girls' red berets, and the girls chased them with exaggerated fuss and kittenish squeals and round-cheeked laughter. The Pagoda was the monument the Korean government had given to Colombia. It wasn't always there: for years it had adorned a busy roundabout, disconcerting passersby who didn't know or had forgotten what the monument commemorated; Salazar passed it every week in the company of his wife, sometimes with his children, and the burden of the questions he hadn't answered never stopped weighing on him, the stories he hadn't wanted to tell. His wife had died at the end of the previous year (cancer, ten months of dying that felt like ten years) without ever knowing anything about the Korean War beyond the official version Colombians had been told, which in broad strokes corresponded to Salazar's. When she asked Salazar something, he answered evasively. "I don't remember," he'd say. "That was so long ago." And she understood, of course, and his children understood as well: when someone has been in a war, when someone has really been in a war and seen the things one sees in war, it's normal not to want to remember them out loud; it's enough to deal with private memories. On those occasions of truncated dialogues, his wife spoke to their children with an admiration and respect not always so readily apparent at other moments of their lives.

"Those poor kids," Trujillo was saying. "They should never have been allowed to go to war."

"Why not?" his wife asked.

"Nor should the reservists," Gutiérrez cut in. "What a disaster the reservists were, they didn't know anything. You should have seen their faces at the weapons presentation. Were you guys at the weapons presentation?"

Ah, the weapons presentation. Yes, Salazar remembered that too: a ceremony for which the entire Colombia Battalion had to travel to Puente de Boyacá—almost two hours in uncomfortable train cars. There, beside the swollen Teatinos River in the rainy season, a stone's throw from the place where Bolívar had won the definitive battle against the Spaniards, right in front of a bronze statue whose trumpet served as a pigeon perch, Monsignor Carmona blessed the troops and especially blessed the 75mm caliber recoilless rifles (a drop of holy water fell on the rifle of a soldier next to him, and Salazar thought it was going to rain again). "You are going to a foreign land," Monsignor Carmona said, "to defend a democracy anointed by the blood of Christ. You are going to defend our families, threatened by the monster of totalitarianism. You are our advance guard, your chests the wall against which our enemies will shatter, enemies of Colombia and the ideals Colombia defends." Later, when they were all walking toward the buses, Salazar heard one officer say to another:

"Well, I don't know if we need to."

"Need to what?"

"Go to the other side of the world to defend our families. We're already killing each other here."

"That's different."

"Then can somebody explain why," the first one said. "The way I see things, it's quite simple: they're sending us far away to get killed so there won't be so many of us they'll have to kill here."

It was already dark when they got back to Bogotá, even though it was barely five o'clock. The journey was long; in the train, in the occasionally perfect darkness of the train, not a word was heard. Each time they passed a lit-up place, a station or a road to a town, the glow sketched the soldiers' stony faces, brought them into the world for a fleeting instant, and it was as if the yellow light created the tense frowns and pursed lips and then returned them to the darkness. Salazar then discovered, with fascination, the various expressions that fear provoked, or rather, the arts fear uses to appear in a certain way of touching one's neck, or leaning one's head to look at the empty back of a seat. And he was thinking about what the officers had said: here, two villages away from the Boyacá bridge, the regime's police cut the throats of their enemies and private armies raped their wives, and meanwhile they were learning that Chosun meant Land of the Morning Calm and that the reason for this monumental mess was what happened in a place that didn't exist: the 38th parallel. A black line on a colored map.

"I was at the weapons presentation," Salazar said.

"Oh, but we didn't see each other there, did we? I don't remember you there. I do remember you at the presentation of the flag. You were there, in the Plaza de Bolívar. Weren't you, Salazar?"

"Weapons presentation, then flag presentation," a woman who hadn't spoken before said. "What a craze for presenting things, no wonder there's nothing left in this country."

"Yes, I was there," Salazar said.

"Who wasn't," Trujillo said. "Even my mother was there."

Everybody laughed.

"Mine too," Gutiérrez said. "And my wife. Who wasn't my wife yet, but my fiancée. But there she was, for the troops' morale."

Only then did Salazar realize that the woman at his left was Gutiérrez's wife.

"For one soldier's morale," she said. "I couldn't have cared less about the troops."

This time there was a histrionic quality to the group's laughter, teeth revealed and hands clasping, and Salazar thought there was something special about this woman, something that provoked subtle courtesies. Because he was standing beside her, he hadn't looked at her closely; now, noticing her hair so blond it resembled well-worn gray, the elegant skin over her cheekbones and her straight back, Salazar had the irresistible impulse to introduce himself, even though they'd been standing beside each other for so long. The woman responded with a firm handshake, and a tinkle of bracelets accompanied her name:

"Mercedes de Gutiérrez," she said with one of those voices that you think you've heard before. "Nice to meet you."

"Now then, we have to tell the truth," Trujillo said. "Doña Mercedes was not there only to accompany her fiancé. Also because her surname demanded it."

"Why demanded?" his wife asked. "What surname?"

Trujillo scowled in exasperation. "Believe it or not," he answered as if speaking to a little girl, "Doña Mercedes is the daughter of General De León, may he rest in peace: hero of the nation and adviser to all presidents since the world began."

"Including the one then," Gutiérrez said.

"Of course," Trujillo said. "Including that one back then." Then he turned to Gutiérrez's wife. "For me it was an honor to know your father, Doña Mercedes. He was everything I wanted to be in the army. It must have been a privilege growing up with a man like him."

"Well, it wasn't so easy," she said. "Imagine: an only child and a daughter at that. I grew up more watched over than a

Russian spy. Sometimes I think I got married to get out of the house."

Nobody looked at Gutiérrez. Trujillo said:

"You two got married after the war, didn't you?"

"I was eighteen when you guys went to Korea," Mercedes said. "We got engaged the day before the flag presentation. We married as soon as you all came back."

Maybe that was why this woman seemed familiar to him, Salazar thought: he had probably seen her there, at the solemn battle-flag presentation ceremony, occupying some prominent place in view of all the soldiers: she beside her father and her father beside the president. The Plaza de Bolívar was packed with soldiers from the garrison, surrounded by government police agents, and on the avenues that frame the square the soldiers' relatives, dressed in their Sunday best, bearing up as well as they could with the persistent drizzle that stung their faces, and enduring the cold, the cold that savaged their wet hands and feet, the cold that slashed at the nape of their necks when the wind blew in those open spaces. From a distance, from his position lost in the green forest of troops, Salazar had seen Lieutenant Gutiérrez approach the Capitol steps to receive the flag from the hands of President Laureano Gómez, and now he understood that maybe the young woman Lieutenant Gutiérrez was going to marry had been there, on the steps. In front of everyone, President Gómez shook the lieutenant's hand, unsmiling and without looking at him, and

Salazar thought it implausible that this lean, resentful-looking man should have enough authority to send a whole country into a world war. The president handed the staff to Lieutenant Gutiérrez; he gripped the wood with both hands, and at that moment a gust of wind came from behind the cathedral and almost snatched it from his grasp. The president said something that Salazar didn't manage to understand and everyone began to clap. The noncommissioned officers flanking the lieutenant stood to attention, and the three of them began to march, at the head of the retinue, toward the Plaza San Diego.

"That's why you seem familiar to me," Salazar said to Mercedes de Gutiérrez.

"Why?"

"Well, an hourlong ceremony . . . Us all lined up there in front of the Capitol, and you there. Because I imagine you were up there."

"I was there for a while."

"We were facing you for an hour, more than an hour. I remember the president, I think I remember General De León. And you look familiar to me, Doña Mercedes. That must be why."

"Well, yes," Mercedes said. "I can't think of any other reason." She paused and added: "Because after that you went to Korea."

"Exactly."

"Like everyone did," Mercedes said.

One of the soldiers who marched beside him that day was a thin, fragile-looking young man, whose helmet seemed too big for his head and whose tie was not properly knotted, so the knot kept slipping and ended up revealing the button of his shirt. Salazar had spoken briefly with him some days earlier, during a break from maneuvers, and had found out his family was also from Boyacá, that he'd been an orphan since the age of ten, that he was planning to pay for his university studies with his earnings from Korea. "Maybe I'll be able to go and study in the United States," the boy had said to him. "If a person distinguishes himself in combat the Gringos pay for your degree, that's what they say." Salazar thought he was a nice kid (he saw him as a kid, despite the fact that the age difference between them must have been minimal). But he didn't see him after that, and only noticed him again ten days later, when the troops left Bogotá in several buses and drove down the mountains toward Buenaventura. There, in the Pacific port, the *Aiken Victory* awaited them, the U.S. troopship that would take them to Korea. Salazar shared a seat with the soldier, and during the trip saw him crying without sound or sobs, just the weeping of fear. The soldier had finally fallen asleep as they drove down into the Cauca River valley, and he was asleep at the moment of the accident: the week's rains had loosened the earth of the hillsides, and the driver lost control on a bend, and the bus skidded on the wet mud that covered the pavement, left the road and crashed, ten yards below, into an adobe wall. There were no fatalities, but there were several serious injuries, and two of the passengers took advantage of the confusion to desert. One of them was the soldier who wanted to go to the United States. The other, whose instinctive decision in the moment of the accident surprised himself more than anyone else, was Salazar.

And now Mercedes, Lieutenant Gutiérrez's wife, had said: *Like everyone did.* Then she offered to bring them all another glass of wine. "I need a drink," she said. "You can't go through so many memories without something to wash them down."

"I'll go with you," Trujillo's wife said.

"There wouldn't be anything a little stronger, maybe a little aguardiente?" Trujillo said.

"I'll ask," his wife said.

And there was that memory now that had so often visited Salazar: he saw himself running through the thick brush on a night of intense rain, his hands in front of him so the invisible branches wouldn't emerge out of the darkness to scratch his face, and as he ran he left behind the lights illuminating the wet trees and making sparks of water burst through the air, and behind him he also left the cries for help and screams of pain. During the following days, which he spent hidden in the woods like a guerrilla while making decisions with a muddled head, Salazar thought he'd been mistaken, then that he'd been completely right, and finally that some of his comrades would come back dead from Korea, and he could say when he read one of their names in a newspaper: *That could have been me.*

And now Mercedes had returned with two glasses in each hand, arranged among the rings on her long fingers, and Salazar admired that license that lightened the solemnity of the moment. Trujillo's wife told him they hadn't found any aguardiente, but here was another glass of wine, and he took it without looking at her while remembering the *Aiken Victory*'s stopover in Honolulu, where the boat's boilers had broken down and forced the crew to stay two days longer than expected. Four of the soldiers, after going to a brothel, got lost in the Hawaiian night, later they showed up drunk by the Kawaiahaʻo Church, had to be transported to Korea in a military plane, and were eventually court-martialed. "I knew one of them," Trujillo said. "He was one of the ones who boarded at Buenaventura. He got killed on Old Baldy, but that's not the sad thing, the sad thing was we all knew since before we left Colombia that he'd get killed. The guy wasn't made for that shit."

"None of you were made for that shit," Mercedes said. "Or, maybe now you're going to tell us you all knew how to fight in snow."

"More than one lost a finger," Gutiérrez said, "for not listening to the Gringos. It's just that snow is something else. Did you have to fight in the snow, Salazar?"

"Yes," Salazar said. "But with the *papasanes.*"

The burst of laughter from the veterans startled other groups. The *papasanes* were the thickset men who presided over the brothels, near the front, where slender Korean girls used empty C-7 shell cases to set up their improvised shacks and sell themselves for fifty cents. Salazar had learned over time at these occasions that a reference to those places was a way of changing the subject, of hiding in plain sight behind masculine complicity. "The ones who talk most are the ones who did the least," a veteran had told him at one of these commemorations, and he had gone through his life like this, on the basis of short, enigmatic phrases, dropping crumbs of information where the others could see a suggestion and fill in the rest of the picture with their own imagination, with their own memories. Sometimes Salazar would drop one of these comments and believe, for a second, that he had really been there, drinking beer and playing Frank Sinatra records on the Gringos' jukeboxes, instead of scraping by with shitty jobs while trying to avoid the war over here.

"Oh, so you were one of those," said Mercedes, who had not only understood the allusion, but had appreciated it with a crooked smile.

"But only in my free time," Salazar said.

And then something happened. On Mercedes's face, over her ironic and delicate smile, a shadow suddenly passed. It was nothing, a play of light on her skin, the color of her gaze: maybe Salazar had imagined it. "Now it really does look like it's going to rain," someone said. Trujillo was talking to Gutiérrez about veterans who'd recently died; Mercedes, the smile gone from her face, was looking at the ground as if she'd lost something in the grass, and on her hardened mouth vertical age lines had appeared. The others had begun to remember the evasion classes, in which more highly trained officers taught them what to do if they were captured by the Chinese; Mercedes was looking for what she'd lost in the grass, a coin, an earring, an uncomfortable memory; her husband was talking about his most dangerous mission, a nighttime patrol during which twenty-five soldiers had to cross an expanse of snowy ground to get to no-man's-land. And it was at that moment, while Gutiérrez was talking about the footsteps you didn't hear in the snow and the fear of running into a Chinese soldier on the other side of the hill, it was at that moment when the group's attention was concentrated on the tale of the night patrol, when Mercedes looked up and Salazar knew she'd found what she was looking for, and it was as if the last fifty years collapsed and she was facing him again, facing Salazar without knowing his name was Salazar, and he without knowing her name was Mercedes, both of them drinking coffee one afternoon in the middle of the last century and letting the hours go by there in a bar full of drunks in downtown Bogotá: a seedy place where Mercedes, despite having covered her head with a black shawl, shone like a jewel.

"What we did find were two dead Chinese," Gutiérrez said. "Dead and frozen."

"And could you see them?" Trujillo asked.

"The searchlight was on," Gutiérrez said, "and there were clouds. It was almost as if dawn were breaking."

It was a strange job he'd gotten, but at that time he hadn't been able to turn it down: Salazar was a young man without education or experience, as well as a deserter. So he found himself, from one day to the next, driving down into the Eastern Plains in a Willys-Overland and walking along the banks of the Guatiquía River carrying a jute sack whose loose fibers scratched the skin on his arms. The routine was always the same and happened once a week: Salazar, with the help of two local boys whom he paid in soda pop, filled the sack with live frogs and returned to Bogotá to sell them for three pesos each to the laboratories downtown. After his second trip, when he dared to ask what the frogs were for, they told him about women who waited twenty-four hours to find out if they were pregnant, and Salazar, who might have been surprised that a frog would start to lay eggs when injected with human urine, instead wondered how so many clients could approach the clinics each week with the same uncertainty. He dropped off the frogs at the labs and collected others, which for incomprehensible reasons hadn't been useful, and crossed the city to get rid of them in the northern wetlands, almost as far as the Común Bridge, where it was easy to leave the Willys without attracting anyone's attention. That's how he made his living for four, maybe five months. He remembered waiting for payment in the laboratory reception rooms, and finding out from the magazines about the latest Colombian deaths and thinking, *That could have been me*; he remembered having been in Villavicencio when the news of Old Baldy began to come in; he remembered later, when the last boat came back from Korea, he was no longer doing that job, but had moved on to the next one, which might have been cleaning the bullring. But he hadn't remembered for many years—decades, maybe—the girl with gray eyes and hair the color of light who approached him one of those days and asked him, with three very large banknotes in hand, if she could trust him.

"In no-man's-land?" Trujillo said. "And you were in command?"

"I had the map, at least," Gutiérrez said. "The idea was to probe as far as the Chinese positions. Twenty-five Colombian soldiers up to their knees in the snow, each with a white jacket and trousers over his uniform. Each with a torch in hand that it wasn't necessary to turn on."

"Because the searchlight was on," Trujillo said.

"Exactly," Gutiérrez said.

Salazar took a quick look around, but didn't see anyone; and that was strange, because the gray-eyed woman was the kind of person who did not tend to walk around downtown

Bogotá on her own, without a friend, without an employee, without a chaperone. He didn't need more explanations to understand, nor did he ask what was in the little jar when he saw it appear in the young woman's hand like a card in a magic act. Someone had already told him in the laboratory about these brazen little women who ended up getting themselves in trouble before their time, and who in other ages would have had to wait weeks for their own blood, or rather its absence, to confirm what they most feared. Now they could find out in a matter of hours. Salazar did not take the jar; the amber liquid remained there, between the two of them, in full view of everyone on Calle Octava in the middle of the day, and the woman had to put it back in the large pocket of her overcoat. "Why don't you take it to the laboratory?"

"That's what I'm paying you for," the woman said. "So you'll take it."

"But I don't work there," Salazar said. "I just take them the frogs."

Clumsily, the woman looked in her black bag and found another banknote. In her eyes there was something pleading, something childish.

"Please," she said.

Gutiérrez was talking about what they did so their steps— the steps of twenty-five soldiers in a quiet night—didn't give them away. "That many people make noise in the snow," he said. He made a theatrical pause in the story, and Trujillo recognized the order. In unison, they shouted like accomplices: "Send me Maruja!" That was the signal: the artillery observer launched a volley to cover their tracks. After that, the enemy was alert.

"And weren't you all scared to death?" Trujillo's wife asked.

"I don't know about the rest of them, but I was," Gutiérrez said.

"My husband has never told me anything like this," Trujillo's wife said.

"Of course I have," said Trujillo. "A thousand times." And then he turned to the others. "But I tell her about maneuvers and she falls asleep halfway through."

"And did they shoot at you?" she asked.

"That was the idea," Gutiérrez said. "The whole operation was designed to detect enemy positions and see what armaments they had. We wanted them to fire on us. We needed them to fire on us."

"How terrifying," Trujillo's wife said.

Salazar returned to the lab, but found it closed for lunch. And he then found himself in an unthinkable situation: eating something in a bar full of drunken workers with a glass of *aguapanela* and a jar of rich girl's urine. He paid with one of his new notes and waited a good quarter of an hour there, looking at the people, until someone left a copy of *Cromos* and Salazar could entertain himself by looking at the photos.

There was a lot about Korea, but Salazar didn't read the news: he stared at the images, memorized impressions, studied the captions; he struggled to imagine himself there. When he arrived at the laboratory, they were just opening. A woman in a white lab coat took the jar and wrote down his surname, and Salazar thought that it was worth more than it ever had been worth: Salazar had rented it out so another person wouldn't have to give her own. "You're the one who brings us the frogs," the woman in the white coat said.

"Yes ma'am," Salazar said.

"I see," the woman said with a little smile that was like a judgment or a taunt. Salazar didn't care; he thought he would have cared if the urine had been his girlfriend's. Then he heard himself ask:

"Can I see?"

"See what?"

"How they do it. I've always brought the frogs, but I've never seen what happens next."

"We never knew what happened next," Gutiérrez said. "These things start without warning."

The firing came from the depths of the night, and kept coming, endlessly, from invisible places, and the soldiers, amid the flashes and thunderous noise, had to spot where the projectiles were falling and at the same time overcome the terror that made them hunch their heads down between their shoulders. The intelligence officers were measuring, observing, and drawing conclusions, and that was what Gutiérrez was risking his life for; but standing there, in the emphatic darkness, up to his knees in white snow, he wasn't thinking of conclusions or measurements, but of how to save his life.

"And also about the fiancée I'd left in Bogotá," he said then. "I was thinking I had to go back home to get married, and not leave her with her wedding dress made and nowhere to wear it."

That was the moment when an explosion right next to him deafened him and the air shook and a whistling began in his ears, and before he could wonder if he'd been injured, the piercing screams of a comrade reached him. He didn't immediately recognize him, because extreme pain disfigures men's voices, but the impact had struck to his right; Gutiérrez followed blindly, for suddenly the night was not as bright or the camp's searchlight had been turned off, or at least that was what it seemed like in the midst of that world jumbled up by fear. "I found him ten yards away, but those ten yards seemed to go on forever," Gutiérrez said. "It was like crossing the whole expanse of ground."

"Who was it?" Trujillo asked.

"It was Yepes," Gutiérrez said. "One of those who'd volunteered at the end, in Buenaventura." He paused and said: "The projectile had blown off his foot."

"How ghastly," Trujillo's wife said.

"They caused us nothing but problems," Trujillo said.

"Those who joined up at the end, I mean. They weren't professional soldiers."

"And what did you do?" Trujillo's wife asked.

"I threw him over my shoulder, what else could I do," Gutiérrez said. "Luckily he was a short kid, and skinny too, pure muscle. Although snow makes everything heavier."

"Your husband is a hero," Trujillo's wife said to Mercedes. Her eyes were wide and she was smiling with admiration. "And how did you hear about this?"

"In the paper," Mercedes said.

"In the *newspaper*?" Trujillo's wife said.

"They gave him a silver star and he was in all the papers," Mercedes said. But her tone of voice had changed.

"Are you feeling all right?" Gutiérrez asked.

"What time is it?" she said. "I have to go home."

"Three o'clock," Salazar said. "The results will be ready in an hour."

"An hour," she repeated.

"Come back later, if you want," Salazar said. "I'll wait for you here."

They were in the same place where Salazar had eaten the previous day, and he realized things hadn't come out as the young lady had planned. She undoubtedly thought they'd meet again in the middle of the street, two anonymous people, and Salazar would hand her the results and each of them would continue on their way. More than uncomfortable, she was irritated: she had also arrived too early, perhaps due to nerves and impatience, and the results weren't ready yet. Yes, that was it: nerves. The woman (but she was just a girl) was pale, or Salazar thought she was, and he also thought he detected a trembling in the hand that held a cigarette to her lips and tried to light it with a slender lighter: a little silver case on the side of which appeared a lion and a legend. The young woman finally managed to light her cigarette; she inhaled deeply and blew out the smoke with a gesture that blended desperation with good manners. "Oh my God," she said, and clutched her head. Curious glances came from neighboring tables. "How did I get myself into this?"

"Into what?" Salazar asked.

"I shouldn't be here," the young woman said. "Here, in this place, sitting with you."

Salazar guessed that he was a couple of years older than she, but he couldn't be sure. He felt a sudden protective urge, an inexplicable interest in the disoriented and solitary young lady's well-being: alone here, in this place, sitting with people like him. *Please don't start crying*, he thought.

"Don't worry," he told her. "In a minute I'll go and pick the thing up from the lab, you wait for me here, or somewhere else if you want. I'll give it to you and we'll never see each other again."

The young woman looked up from her hands, and Salazar

saw the gray eyes again. They were upset, sad under her arched brows, but she wasn't crying.

"You're a good person," she said. "Thank you."

"Do you want me to tell you how they do it?"

"What?"

Salazar didn't really know why: maybe to fill the silence, because silence seemed to be this nervous woman's enemy. But he heard himself talking about the frogs he had seen the previous afternoon: their white bellies, their bulging eyes that didn't change when the needle entered their soft bodies. The woman made a disgusted expression, and from the disgust came a little girl's giggle. "Don't tell me that, how horrible," she said, and Salazar kept telling her about the needle that entered the damp skin and the tag they then put on the frog's leg, or maybe they call it the haunch, so they wouldn't confuse it with another frog: imagine the disaster if that happened. And then, they wait one day. But it seems, Salazar began to say, that soon they won't even have to wait that long, because there are people doing experiments—

"My husband is in Korea," the woman interrupted him. "Well, he's not my husband, he's my fiancé." And then: "Him over there, risking his life to save the world, and me in this mess."

"Is he at the front?"

"I'm unforgivable."

"Is he at the front?" Salazar insisted. "The Colombian troops went as occupation forces. Is he at the front?"

"I don't know where he is," the young woman said, "but they just gave him a medal. A star, I think. It was in the papers."

"I didn't know," Trujillo said. "I should have known about that, but I didn't."

"A person can't hear everything," Gutiérrez said.

"So many years and one still gets surprises," Trujillo said. "That's why I like coming to the commemorations."

"And how was your reception?" Trujillo's wife asked. "How does a hero get received?"

"Well," Gutiérrez said, "we all got a hero's welcome. Do you know why? Because we were the last to arrive."

"But in your case there was something more," she said.

"We'd won the war," Trujillo said. "The Colombians—"

"What I'll never forget," Gutiérrez interrupted, "are the rows of mothers. From Buenaventura to Cali, all the mothers came out to see if their sons had come back. And some of them hadn't, of course, and were never going to. And nobody had told them."

"Poor things," the woman said.

"We arrived in Bogotá, fell in, and marched to the Plaza de Bolívar," Trujillo said. "I'll never forget the music."

"'The Bridge on the River Kwai,'" Salazar said. "That's what the band played to welcome us."

Mercedes looked up then. It was a brusque movement: a

doll suddenly galvanized. Salazar looked into her eyes and saw in them, in those gray eyes, something he hadn't seen before.

"Oh yeah?" she spat out. "And how would you know?"

She immediately regretted it; pressed her lips together as if fearing other imprudent comments would slip out. That one had slipped out, however, and there it was, in front of everyone.

Salazar did not say, as he would have said on other occasions, that he remembered it well: he remembered the melody soldiers had whistled in so many other wars, the real name of which was the "Colonel Bogey March," but which the Korean vets had gotten used to associating with a film that had arrived in Colombia when the war was already a memory. He didn't say any of this, but kept quiet like someone holding his breath while a wild beast goes past. The gray eyes hated him: they hated him for knowing what he knew. The gray-eyed woman hated him for never having been in Korea, for having stayed to sell frogs, for having come out of one of the downtown labs one afternoon with results in his hand, for having gone into a seedy place that smelled of wet ponchos and felt hats and where she was waiting with her elbows on the table and her hands over her mouth, and she hated him for not having left when she opened the envelope with the results and saw on the paper the prettiest word in the world, the only word she wanted to see at that moment, the word that returned her life to her and allowed her to start over or rather carry on as if nothing had happened. She hated him for having stayed in the bar, standing beside the rough wooden table, accompanying her and supporting her, and she hated him despite having asked him herself for his company and support, because she didn't feel capable of doing that alone. And she hated him, Salazar thought, for having witnessed the relief on her face and for having received her embrace, her inappropriate embrace, the hug the young woman would never have given him if she'd known she'd ever see him again.

"Oh, sorry," Mercedes said then. "You were in the war too, of course."

"Yes ma'am," Salazar said. "I was there. I didn't come back with a silver star, like your husband, but I was there."

"Don't get offended, Salazar," Gutiérrez said. "She didn't mean—"

"And when I got back I marched down Calle 13, like your husband. And I whistled 'The Bridge on the River Kwai,' like your husband."

"But why are you getting so worked up?" Gutiérrez said.

The sky had darkened and the marquees began to empty out: the veterans and their families were walking toward the parking lot, and a silence, the silence of open spaces, blew between them. There were no longer any little Korean girls in front of the Pagoda; there were no longer groups in animated conversation. *It's been so many years*, Salazar thought: so many years of pretending, of distorting, of remembering eloquent details, details able to deactivate skepticism before it even arises. Then he felt an intense weariness fall on him, across his shoulders, a weariness as heavy as a body we drag through the night and through the snow.

"No," he heard himself say then.

"No what?"

"No, I didn't march down Calle 13," Salazar said.

"Let's go, love," Mercedes said.

"No, I didn't whistle the tune with the rest of you."

"I'm tired," Mercedes said. "Can we please go?"

"I don't understand," Trujillo said. "What do you mean?"

And suddenly Salazar glimpsed the possibility of relief. But it wasn't just the relief of the truth that he was going to reveal even though next would come the fall, but something that could only be power: the power of taking others with him, of dragging them so they would go over the cliff with him, to see as he fell all those lives of heroic memories, like that fabled suicide who threw himself off a roof and as he was falling he saw into his neighbors' lives, saw them through their lighted windows. In the fable, the glimpse of other people's lives, with their laughter and solace and trivial happiness, convinced the poor man that taking his life had been a mistake, but this revelation arrived too late, when death on the pavement below was already inevitable.

Salazar felt sorry for that nonexistent man. And then he heard himself speak.

BAD NEWS

I met him in Paris, in June 1998, in circumstances that didn't give any clues to what would come later. The World Cup finals were being played in France, and the Parisian municipal government had set up a giant screen in the Place de l'Hôtel de Ville, a space normally so tranquil they held book signings and exhibitions of paintings there. The concert speakers flanking the screen were vomiting noise, but this noise could barely be heard: it was drowned out by the shouting of fans and the traffic on the avenues. I hadn't gone with the intention of watching the match—Iran and the United States: I wasn't really interested in either of those teams—and, in fact, I hadn't gone with any intention whatsoever, or my steps had led me to that place as they might have led me to any other. At that time my life in Paris had begun to deteriorate and the city was turning into a hostile creature; it would take a long time, many years of living in other places and of conversations with other people, for me to understand that it wasn't the city that had changed, but I, and that Paris is one of those places that gives us back what we give: a wonderful, open, and generous city for someone who's winning (in love, in work), but cruel and humiliating for those who fail. I was failing: now it strikes me as obvious, but back then it didn't seem so evident: we have lavish mechanisms to reject this kind of evidence. I began to spend my days on the street and in cafés, to let my time go by on walks or drinking glasses of cheap wine with the sole aim of not being alone in my apartment. I got used to starting up conversations about nothing with strangers. I discovered a certain talent for getting people to tell me things; I also discovered that something about me made people trust me, that others felt comfortable with me almost as soon as they met me, and that I liked this new sensation. Before I knew it I was seeking out conversations just to feel it again, just to feel comfortable and appreciated in a city that (I believed) had begun to hate me.

That's what happened that day, the day of the match. I had joined the crowd that was watching the screen; soon the crowd ended up ejecting me, and I decided to give up and have a beer while, against all predictions, Iran scored two goals against the United States and were winning a match that was far more than what it seemed to be. I got to see the last goal, that fruitless U.S. goal, on a television behind the bar, a small set hastily perched on a shelf so the customers would keep drinking instead of going to watch the match in the square. And when the referee blew the final whistle, the customer beside me at the bar, a man of about forty whose English was obviously North American and almost certainly Southern, said out loud: "Serves you right." And I, who've always felt a sort of unspoken bond with those who rail against their own countries, immediately struck up a conversation with him.

As so many people who live alone in a place that's not their own tend to do, we began by exchanging discontents. I told him about the reasons I'd come to Paris, about the two years I'd spent living in the city, about the reasons I now wanted to leave; I told him why I didn't want to go back to Colombia and why the freedom to choose where to live did not seem like a blessing to me, but the most terrible of burdens. He told me he'd come to Paris as he might have gone anywhere. He had just spent three years in Rota, he explained; when I interrupted him to ask what Rota was, he took a pen out of his pocket, turned over a paper place mat, and drew a map of Spain of insolent perfection (in the outline of its coasts, in the odd corners of its borders, even in its shape angled to respect the compass rose), and then, when the cartography exercise was finished, he put one finger on a tiny spot in the south, between Cádiz and a speck of fly shit. Only then, when I realized I was facing one of those men who drew perfect maps almost without lifting the tip of his pen from the paper, I noticed the impeccably ironed jacket, the neurotically close shave, the severe haircut—the right angle of his sideburns as if drawn with the same pen that had sketched the map. He was a soldier. Then John Regis told me his life story, and in doing so he simply filled up the empty receptacle I had unintentionally constructed. There are people who don't hide anything, who carry all that they are in their way of talking or saying hello or lighting a cigarette. I thought John Regis was one of those people. It's not hard to understand why I was so mistaken.

The Rota military base is one of the largest the United States has in Europe, John Regis explained. He told me about it in words as exaggerated as his gestures: the base had the best hospital in Europe, the longest runway in Europe (essential to land the C-5s, the largest airplane in Europe). In the middle of 1995, at the same time as I was finishing my law degree in Bogotá, John Regis arrived at Rota from a base in South Carolina the name of which I didn't manage to catch. He was a helicopter pilot, and he carried documentation of that fact with him, as if he were used to talking to strangers in bars and proving irrefutably the things he told them: he showed me a folded photo someone had taken of him in a hangar, where he appeared with his shirt open and his face bathed in the light from the flash (the dazzling glare made everything it illuminated stand out against a perfectly black background), leaning against the open door of a Sikorsky, not posing, but looking tired. John Regis spoke of his helicopter with obvious affection: he almost seemed to be stroking its nose with his words, as if it were an old horse. In the photo you could see inside the Sikorsky, the radar screens and the seat of the man who operated the radar, and the ample space to fit in an injured or sometimes dead man. John Regis knew this well, of course, because he himself had put a dead man (once) and an injured man (seventeen times) into that space. "That's what I've spent these years doing," John Regis told me. "Saving the lives of irresponsible surfers." And then he put a finger on the map, pointing to the coast near Tarifa: the place where irresponsible surfers go and end up defeated by the power of the waves and lost in the middle of the sea, trembling with fear and cold and full of promises never to do that again.

And we spent quite a while like that: him telling me anecdotes about rescues and me listening, him talking about the cable that descends from the helicopter to the water and me seeing the cable, him explaining that the surfer must never touch the cable before it reaches the water, due to the risk of electrocution . . . And later we talked about other things, and later still others. We talked about Andrés Escobar, a murdered soccer player, and then about Monica Lewinsky, an intern who didn't smoke cigars, and while we talked, drinks came and went. At some point, between a couple of those drinks, John Regis mentioned, for no apparent reason, the name of one of his best friends in Rota, a guy called Peter Semones. So he started to tell me things that somehow came from the ones he'd already told me, that weren't gratuitous or lacking pertinence, but that nevertheless forced me to wonder more than once why he was telling me these things.

Peter Semones was one of the most talented pilots who had ever been stationed at any of the European bases. Nobody knew a Sikorsky better than Peter Semones did. The helicopters were his friends, and Peter Semones took care of them like the old horse I'd thought I'd seen in the photo of John Regis. Peter Semones, John Regis was telling me, took it upon himself to look out for the kites and owls that nested in the rafters of the hangars, to make sure no one disturbed their nests, so those owls and kites would swoop down once in a while and eat the field mice and small birds that otherwise would get into the turbines, would eat the wire casings, would destroy, with their corrosive shit, the delicate materials of which the motors were made. Regis spoke of that man with frank admiration; I got the idea of a burly blond like the marines in movies, but Regis didn't have any photos of him, so I couldn't be sure. I did find out, however, that Peter Semones still held the record for escaping from the pool, a blue box filled with water into which they dropped pilots locked up as if they were latter-day Houdinis; I found out that he was the only one never to hesitate before climbing aboard a number thirteen craft, in spite of the fact that experience, not superstition, had demonstrated that number thirteens went down— the verb worked like that, impersonal, irresponsible—more often than others.

I found all that out. But I also found out other things, and while I was finding them out I kept asking myself the same question: *Why? Why is he telling me these things?* I found out, for example, that Peter Semones was married. His wife was a former beauty queen from Minneapolis. Laura was her name, and she had freckles on her chest, and in her few years on the Rota military base she had invented a perfect routine, a simulated sham that passed for real life. At the Rota base, life is fictitious, John Regis told me: Episcopalian churches, theaters with Hollywood movies that hadn't yet been released in Europe, outdoor screens as if the residents were couples from the 1950s, making out in convertibles, diners where they served pizza and hamburgers twenty-four hours a day, arcades with slot machines and video games a couple of steps away from the diners, golf courses, baseball diamonds, American football fields. A parallel world, John Regis said: and Laura Semones lived there, oblivious of the village of Rota, oblivious of Andalusia and of Spain, oblivious of the fact of not living in the United States. As if her house had been carried off by a tornado, John Regis said, and dropped there, in unknown territory. Laura Semones as a modern version of Dorothy, the girl from *The Wizard of Oz*. Dorothy, without a little dog or a witch or a yellow brick road.

"We were very close friends," John Regis said. "Then not so much. We grew apart a bit. That was before the accident."

That was how John Regis told me that Peter Semones was

dead. But why, why did he tell me? He wanted to tell me; it was, I thought, as if he'd stayed after the match to tell someone about the death of Peter Semones, and I had been the lucky beneficiary of this haphazard intention, of that lottery whose prize was the tale of Peter Semones's death. Yes, I thought, it was meant to be. What most struck me was that not even a month had passed since his friend's death: it was fresh, still able to make his hands tremble (no, nothing to do with the Four Roses we'd begun to order unabashedly), still able to make John Regis bow his head slightly when talking about it (when we talk about the death of someone we respect, any place is transformed into a confessional). Or perhaps, deep down, what struck me was the faintness of the trembling, how slight the inclination of his head—in short, the control John Regis seemed to have already gained over such a recent death. The circumstances of which, furthermore, were not surrounded by the aura of peace or rest that surrounds some deaths, for Peter Semones, the great pilot, the Houdini of the practice pool, had been burnt to death during a routine summer operation, when his helicopter crashed into a burning mountain.

"We'd spent the week talking about things like that," John Regis told me. "Wondering if it would be our turn one day, what we'd feel if it happened to us." During heat waves there were always forest fires, John Regis explained, and the people from *Protección Civil*—these two words he said in Spanish—always ended up needing help or support from the Rota helicopters and their Yankee pilots. That was what had happened this time: the heat had settled over the Mediterranean early, and all over the place, in all the mountains of Andalusia, fires began to break out like oil lamps smashing against the ground. Where there was a tree to burn, a stubborn fire encouraged by the winds would flare up, a fire fed by pine needles and dry bark like an inoffensive Boy Scout campfire. One weekend, John Regis and two other pilots had flown to Málaga to oversee operations from those hangars, closer to the fire, and Málaga received the report that one of the three pilots had gone down. Several minutes of uncertainty passed before confirmation arrived, the definite identity of the dead pilot, and John Regis experienced once more the terrible sensation of wishing for someone's death: because wishing for his friend's salvation was, implicitly, to condemn one of the pilots who weren't friends of his. "I can hear it as if I had it right here," said John Regis. "The static, the kid's voice over the wire. I can hear all that, but I can also hear the silence in the hangar. I can hear the heat. Is that possible? I don't know if it's possible." It was the heat that Peter Semones must have felt, John Regis would say to himself later, imagining his friend's body destroyed by the crash into the forest and pitilessly devoured by the flames.

"And his wife?"

"It was up to me," John Regis said. "I had to go and give her the news."

And this is what he told me—but why, why did he tell me? He told me how he had returned to Rota from Málaga thinking about Laura Semones the whole time, trying to think of her in order not to think about Peter's burnt and broken body. He told me he'd been tempted to go into the movie theater where *Armageddon* was showing and stay there forever, eternally watching Ben Affleck and Liv Tyler sing that song, *I'm leavin' on a jet plane, Don't know when I'll be back again*, and letting the world bring Laura Semones the news of the death of her husband. He told me how he'd walked, in the cruel heat, along those streets with names of flowers and trees, passing in front of identical houses, all with the peaceful white walls of an American suburb, all with their mailboxes and each mailbox with its little red flag, all with their Chevrolet or their Chrysler in the carport and some with a tricycle or a skateboard parked right alongside the Chrysler or the Chevrolet. He told me how from a distance he had seen the silhouette of Laura Semones, who was watering plants in her garden with a green hose, and how he had seen her disappear behind the house and reappear with a bag in her hands. He told me how when he reached her yard he'd realized the bag was full of seeds, and that Laura was planting them in the furrow that served as the border between her house and her neighbor's. He told me how he told her what he had to tell her, almost without saying hello, without asking her to sit down or any of those phrases people say in movies, and John Regis would always remember the image of the bag of seeds falling to the ground and the seeds spilling around Laura's feet, beside the sleeping hose, and Laura bursting into tears, holding her face in her hands without noticing they were covered in dirt, so after, when John Regis hugged her somehow—mainly to keep her from fainting and hurting herself by falling—he felt bits of soil on his own face that were stuck in Laura's hair and on her cheek, black soil, an intense black, artificial soil you'd be hard-pressed to find naturally along this stretch of the Spanish coast.

Years went by and I didn't think of John Regis again. I didn't think about our farewell (a big hug, as if we were friends) when I left Paris; I didn't think of him (or his promises to write) in October 1999, when I moved to Barcelona; I didn't think of him (or of Peter Semones, the dead pilot) in August 2007, when by chance a family holiday took me to Málaga. But once I was there, nothing was more natural than recovering the memory of that summer in Paris and thinking of John Regis again, nine years after meeting him, and nothing more natural, after remembering that conversation and explaining it a couple of times to my wife and my friends, than giving in to the temptation of hiring a car one morning and driving the three hours from Málaga to Rota, not with the idea of seeing him—it seemed unlikely he would still be living there—but of seeing firsthand the curious spectacle of a military base larger than the town next to it. Tourist: that would be my occupation in Rota. The worst that could happen, I thought, would be that I'd end up sitting in a bar or a café asking people questions (the people of Rota know the presence of the base has improved their lives more than anyone could have foreseen, and have always felt divided between gratitude and the notion that the base is, ultimately, a foreign body), and then maybe I'd write a short article for some magazine, which would offset the day's expenses. But I was secretly hoping that a stroke of luck would enable me to get onto the base: I was hoping the young soldiers who guarded the entrance to the base under the brutal sun would surrender in the face of my books, which I'd brought along as identification, or at least in the face of my press pass, even though it had expired. Of course, it didn't happen that way: the books did not impress them in the slightest, they didn't even look at the pass, and all they did was point out to me, not without courtesy, that entrance was forbidden. It was futile to insist, I thought; but I insisted and discovered, as was to be expected, the futility of doing so. And that was when I decided to look for John Regis.

I called directory inquiries. The woman who answered did not have an Andalusian accent. We have no listing for anyone by that name, she told me.

I repeated the surname, spelling it out carefully, assigning each letter a place name, as I've seen people do: Rota, Ecuador,

Geneva, Iceland, Switzerland. There is no listing for anyone by that name, the woman repeated (she was Latin American) from the other end of the line. We have no customer with that name.

Suddenly annoyed, I got in the car and headed for the road leading to the motorway that would take me back to Málaga. But I was annoyed not because I hadn't found John Regis, but by the fact that not finding him surprised me: I was annoyed by my own naiveté. I began to drive around the base, seeing the ocean in the distance, imagining the troopships in the port, believing the glints I was seeing were caused by the sun shining on masts or radar dishes. The road went on and on and so did the barbed wire of the base, the deterring structures enclosing a wasteland, all covered in short grass, the only function of which was to demarcate the military installations from civilian life. I began to wonder what had become of John Regis: if he'd ever returned to the Rota base, if he was still in Europe, if someone had met him during the 2002 World Cup, watching one of the USA's matches in a café somewhere. Now there was something resembling frustration in my failure: it was suddenly frustrating not to be able to see the swimming pool Peter Semones escaped from with extraordinary ease, or to go inside the hangars where there were owls that ate field mice so the mice wouldn't eat the cables of the turbines. And that's what I was doing, remembering the details of a conversation I'd had with that stranger who wasn't one in a city that hadn't been strange and now was, remembering with something like shame the almost suicidal way John Regis had confessed to me (with that frankness someone you'll never see again can have), that's what I was doing, as I said, when I wondered for the first time what had become of Laura Semones. And without stopping the car, simply checking in the rearview mirror to make sure no police car was sneaking up on me, I got out my phone and dialed the number for directory inquiries. Switzerland, Ecuador, Madrid, Oslo, Nicaragua, Ecuador, Switzerland. "Do you want me to put you through?" the operator said. And in a matter of seconds I'd made an illegal U-turn and was driving back into Rota, speaking on the phone with Laura Semones and telling her, for some unknown reason, a white lie. No, it wasn't even a lie, barely an exaggeration, a slight distortion: that I was a friend of John Regis, that John had told me a lot about her, that I'd love to meet her.

"So, you were a friend of Johnny's," Laura Semones said.

I tried to guess her age: forty, forty-five. Laura Semones spoke Spanish with a curious blend of Andalusian and North American consonants, aspirated *s*'s and drunken *r*'s; and she was, I can confirm, a former beauty queen. There were the freckles that John Regis had described; but Regis had not described the sureness of her bearing, the solidity of her handshake (despite so many years in Spain, she had not acquired the habit of saying hello with kisses on the cheek at first meeting). In her voice and gestures, in the way she moved around her tiny apartment, there was something that could only be called maturity. Maturity in an action as banal as offering me a can of San Miguel from the fridge; maturity in setting a green glass down on the clear glass of the coffee table. "So how is Johnny?" she asked.

"I don't know," I said. "I haven't seen him for a while."

"Ah. Well, me neither. Better that way." And then: "How do you know each other?"

I didn't have too many options: I told her about Paris, I told her about the Place de l'Hôtel de Ville, I told her about the soccer match. I told her about the long night when John Regis—Johnny, I said—had told me about the accident, about the thankless task that had fallen to him. "It wasn't easy for him," I said, already up to my neck in the role I was playing and not really knowing why I was doing it, what I thought I'd get out of it. But then Laura Semones asked me, genuinely perplexed, what I was referring to; and I must have blushed a little as I spoke about John Regis arriving at the house on the base and the bag of seeds that Laura Semones had in her hands when she received the news of the accident. But, blushing and all, I did not expect the ominous half smile that was breaking out on Laura's face, a smile of painful irony, which didn't invite a reciprocal smile, but rather inspired fear. "He said that?"

"You dropped the bag," I said. "The two of you embraced."

"I dropped the bag," Laura Semones repeated. "We hugged." She waited a moment, looking like she might burst into tears, like she might go straight from the fearsome smile into uncontrolled wailing. And then she said three simple words, and from her lips they sounded even shorter than they actually are: "What a bastard."

I remember how hot it was when Laura Semones began to tell me what had really happened. I remember, as well, the drops of condensation on the beer can starting to form a little puddle on the glass tabletop. Later I would ask myself again, like an echo of other encounters, why she had told me all that, or what for, but this time it was a hypocritical question: I had this answer, this time I did know why she'd told me, or what she told me for. To put a mistaken emotion in its place; to banish from her memory any remains of affection that might have been stuck in there. "Do you know the houses on the base?" Laura Semones asked me. I said yes (another lie, of course). "Well," Laura continued, "ours was beside the school. During the day you could hear the commotion of the children playing, shouting, bouncing balls. That's all year round, except on weekends and holidays. And that day was a Sunday. I don't like air-conditioning, I've never liked it, so I had the windows open, and I was there, sitting in my living room, enjoying the silence of the street without the children, when John arrived.

He didn't ring the bell, instead he leaned in the open window. As soon as I saw him I knew what he'd come for. So I closed the window, opened the door, and didn't even wait for him. I started taking my clothes off as I was walking upstairs, to save time. When I got to the bed all I had on was a white skirt Peter had brought me back from Morocco one time. And like that, with my skirt still on, without having exchanged a single word, I went to bed with Johnny."

It was the second time they'd done it. The first had been the previous winter, a drunken accident: festive season, Laura Semones said, Peter away on training, feeling neglected, a silly fight, desire for revenge. "As soon as it happened I told Johnny it had been a mistake, that it wasn't going to happen again," Laura Semones said. "He agreed without complaining, because he loved him too. Peter was his friend. He'd taught him stuff." But the weeks went by and it wasn't so easy to maintain that situation: when they got together with friends, went to the movies (John Regis was always there), their mutual attraction was troubling and inescapable. "We touched each other under the table, silly adolescent things," Laura Semones said. "If Peter was away on maneuvers, Johnny would come over and spend time here, listening to music with me, and maybe we'd kiss, but it never went any further. I don't know, we were scared, or I was scared. What can I say. Deep down I knew it was going to happen again, I'm not an idiot. Later I threw that skirt away, obviously. But first we went to the movie theater. In that order: sex, movie, and then I threw the skirt away."

"To the movies?" I asked.

"Johnny told me there wasn't any risk, that Peter wasn't going to get back yet. I asked him: Are you sure? And he said: Yeah, I'm sure. And we went to see a movie. *Armageddon*. That I'll never forget. The one about the meteorite and the astronauts."

"The one with the song."

"Yeah, did you see it? *I'm leavin' on a jet plane*," Laura Semones sang. "That song was playing and Johnny, sitting beside me, knew perfectly well that my husband had just been killed. It still seems incredible."

He never did tell her: John Regis never gave her the news he had to give her. They said good night like friends outside the theater, and Laura Semones walked home alone and happy, not yet able to feel guilty for what she'd done, humming the song from the movie. Waiting for her, on the answering machine, were four messages. It took her a while to understand the first one, because she was missing a piece of information: the piece that John Regis was supposed to give her. "We're so sorry, dear," said the voice of a vice admiral of a frigate who was a very good friend of her husband. "We don't want to bother you, but call us if there's anything you need." And then three more messages. While she was listening to them, as she gradually realized what had happened (though not the details), Laura remembered, incredulous, John's arrival. In some shameful and contradictory way she actually felt flattered by that man who had been able to maintain a cruel and even violent silence just to sleep with her one last time, knowing that afterward, when she found out about Peter's death, a ghost would come between the two lovers forever. Then she heard, in the distance, the sound of a helicopter, and wondered if it was John Regis taking off, following the long-standing pilot's tradition when one of their own went down: go up and fly as soon as possible, fly to frighten off fear, fly to neutralize death.

Two days after his disappearance, when his ex-wife's anxious questions began to circulate on social media, his friends all agreed that Sandoval, after saying goodbye to us, had gone to see his new girlfriend, an indefatigable twentysomething with tattooed ankles he'd been going out with for a few months, and it wasn't improbable that the night would have gotten out of hand and ended up in some permissive hotel, among empty rum bottles and bare feet kicking them and ghosts of cocaine on glass tables. (His friends knew these kinds of excesses, tolerated them and sometimes judged them: hypocritically, since we'd all participated in them at least once or twice.) But on social media it quickly became obvious that nobody had seen him, not the new girlfriend, not his mother or the neighbors, and the last thing anyone had heard was from a taxi driver who'd waited for him first thing in the morning in front of a north-end bank, yellow door open like a wing and motor running, while Sandoval withdrew more bills than seemed advisable for a person to carry in our relentless city. People thought he'd been kidnapped; they talked about the *millionaire's stroll*, and we had to imagine Sandoval traveling around the city and withdrawing from the cash machines as much money as his generous card limits would allow, and then returning on foot, terrified but safe, from some unfathomable wasteland along the Bogotá River. Social media also brought us messages of solidarity or help, descriptions of Sandoval—five-foot-nine, very short prematurely graying hair—and good wishes written with words that were not optimistic, it's true, but not yet tragic; however, some were already suggesting scenes in which his attackers had followed Sandoval from the bank, waiting to catch him alone and steal his money, his watch, and his cell phone before shooting him in the head.

Alicia, Sandoval's ex-wife, worried from the start more intensely, or at least more publicly, than we would have expected. They had met at university, shortly before Sandoval dropped out, and in their marriage there was something like a subtle imbalance, for she always seemed to be towing him along. It was her idea that Sandoval should set up an investment firm, and she was the one who brought in the first clients and hired the best accountants, she was the one who found the shared office space, to save on expenses, and who convinced Sandoval that it didn't matter if the office was old, since an atmosphere

of plate glass and wood tables smelling of furniture glue wasn't
a problem if people left the office with more money than they
had when they'd arrived. Everyone always thought Alicia deserved someone better than Sandoval, and the first hours of
his disappearance were moving because of that: seeing her, a
woman who was much more solid than he was, more worldly
and much more lively, using all the force of her sadness to
worry about a guy like our friend: unstable, evasive, always on
the move, as if someone were chasing him.

Then we learned that the banknotes had safely reached
their destination. "The cash was to pay us," his most recent
secretary said later, when the interrogations started. At about
half past eight, the woman had arrived at work to find envelopes with the names of the eleven employees written in the
boss's hand (those backward-leaning letters, as if struggling
through a headwind); later it was revealed that Sandoval had
not just paid them for the current month but the next two as
well, and that was enough to make many on social media
claim he had already made a decision, although nobody knew
the nature of it. About what happened from that moment
on—the *cash machine moment*, as it immediately became
known—nothing was known either; Alicia kept us informed
of the investigations, of the reports made to baby-faced, bored
police officers, of the fruitless searches first of the hospitals
and then of the morgues, and also of the anguish of little
Malena, who had noticed everything and begun to cry

clandestine tears under her tulip blanket. And we wrote to each other deep into the night, simply to share the insomnia of uncertainty.

On the third day after his disappearance, the meticulous social networks brought us a piece of news that confirmed the vilest suspicions: Sandoval had left the country. The pressure of tweets eventually reached the proper ears, and a benevolent magazine revealed on the internet some images of precarious quality in which Sandoval, or someone who looked very much like Sandoval, approached an Immigration window and raised his head, as if to crack the bones in his neck, while a border guard was stamping his passport. We'll never know if at some moment he really thought he could go unnoticed, but it's quite probable he did, because otherwise he would have made more of an effort to hide. On social media an argument soon got under way between two sides: if Sandoval was fleeing from something, some said, he would have disguised himself, would have hidden, would have worn a jacket with a hood or a base-ball cap or a broad-brimmed *vallenato* hat or at least a pair of dark glasses to conceal his face from impertinent and ubiquitous cameras; that he hadn't done so, others held, was simply proof that he believed himself and always had believed himself to be above the law, an untouchable, an owner-of-everything, a member of that class that had been raised with the profound conviction that the country was an enormous estate and they were the overseers.

Alicia wore herself out in vain appeals for respect. She claimed (we saw her claim) that nobody had proof that he'd done anything wrong and in any case there still hadn't been any sign of him, even if she'd seen what the cameras had seen. The family then issued a statement to announce that Sandoval was still officially missing, since, in spite of having *tried all possible means of getting in touch with him,* neither his ex-wife, nor his mother, nor his friends had received any kind of news, *nor had he acknowledged receipt of any of our messages.* Some on social media were already insulting him for his lack of consideration, for seeing the spectacle of his relatives' anguish and not reacting in any way, and others wondered how he was supposed to react, if by this point he was probably in the boot of a car with a bullet in his head. The authorities answered the family's statement with a statement of their own, in which they put on record that Señor Sandoval Guzmán had passed through Immigration at El Dorado International Airport at 7:14 a.m., boarded flight 246, and landed in Washington at 2:39 local time, though they were as yet unable to determine whether he had gone through immigration procedures at Dulles. But as soon as they found out, the statement charitably said, they would reveal the news.

Washington? What reason could Sandoval have for traveling to Washington? Never, as far as our memories of his life went back, had we heard him mention Washington as one of his business destinations, nor could Alicia remember him having any friends or interests there. In a matter of hours new social media groups had started up with names like Support for Sandoval Guzmán in the United States, or Have You Seen Sandoval Guzmán? And there they published photos of men who looked like Sandoval; declarations of Colombians who gave advice (whom to turn to, where to look for him) from their experience as residents in the District of Columbia; theories of what might have happened to him included being in a coma, amnesia, and robbery using scopolamine, which puts people's will at the service of their attackers and whose victims can move, board planes, and show their passports without anyone noticing they are absent from their own bodies. Someone said they'd seen him in a stadium, someone talked to him in a bar, someone was on a bus with him heading south. And on social media we talked about poor Malena and speculated about her, about what could be going through her head, about what answers Alicia would be giving her (and we wondered how much truth would fit in those explanations, how much fabrication was necessary). But we never responded to an anonymous tweet: *Also the guy has an adorable daughter, called Manuela, real sonuvabitch abandoning her like that.* No, we never responded, or corrected the name: it was just a few letters, and it wouldn't have done any good. We did say to each other, though, that Malena was only four, so she would soon forget all of this. But it was also true that on the internet nothing is forgotten, and all this will still be available in ten or fifteen years for the girl, who by then will no longer be a girl, to consult and find out. Because social networks don't forget anything; only good news, satisfactions, and small or large successes are ephemeral on them, while mistakes and guilt and different blunders and careless words, all these things stain a life, remain alert, crouching and ready to jump out in front of us. The stain does not disappear, can never be completely washed away, though we can hide or disguise it, and it only needs to come into contact with the right substances to resurface again on the pristine fabric of our life.

The news began to circulate during the night. It was the first thing we saw in the morning, which for some began before the sun rose. Sandoval had turned up dead in a hotel room, in Jacksonville, in the state of Florida. It seemed he'd arrived there by bus from Washington, passing through Raleigh and Fayetteville and Savannah, on an eighteen-hour trip with no known destination. In the hotel he ordered a hamburger and a glass of wine, and after he'd eaten he'd put the tray with the leftovers out in the hall beside door number 303; and then in pencil he'd filled in the breakfast request form, the one you must hang outside before a certain hour so someone will wake up the guest with their food. He put crosses in the boxes for coffee and orange juice and fried eggs sunny-side up; in the box for serving time, he ticked 7:30. And then, in his underwear and T-shirt, he got in between the sheets and swallowed a jar of sleeping pills with a bottle of water from the minibar. The television was on when they found him, but nobody knew what program he'd been watching when he fell asleep. We would find out in time, of course, each one of the details would come to light, but what has still not been revealed, what is still debated (sometimes in very bitter terms: discussions on the internet are heated), are what reasons Sandoval had to flee from his life. For now we could only speculate, as has been happening for some time: embezzlement, proof of unforgivable promiscuity? Will photos of underage girls now appear, obscene text messages, images of erect penises with shameful captions? Or will we maybe discover some sort of dispossession, an irremediable injustice, the condemnatory results of a medical exam, a sentence that could not be appealed? On this we were agreed, at least: it was an escape Sandoval was carrying out or trying to carry out, a reinvention, the start of a new life. He tried to vanish to become someone else or someone new or to leave without bothering anybody, and it's a shame we hadn't found him in time, for we might have been able to rescue him, yes, persuade him to come back among us.

AIRPORT

I think it was in September 1998, or maybe October, but dates get mixed up in my head these days and I can't be sure these things didn't happen just before the summer. I was still living in Paris and, although I didn't know it yet, I was about to leave the city, partly due to the difficulty of finding ways to earn a living. I had published a 120-page novel with a small Colombian publisher the year before, and the one I was then trying to write would appear the following year, but I was getting by on a student's budget. Those were my circumstances when I received, one Friday, a call that at first I had trouble understanding: someone was talking about next Sunday, about a café in northern Paris, about a bus that would be waiting at seven in the morning, and only then did I remember that M, my girlfriend, had been at the Librería

Española on Rue de Seine a few weeks earlier, and saw a little white paper on the bulletin board that said:

MEN AND WOMEN 25–30 YEARS OF AGE

MEDITERRANEAN APPEARANCE

REQUIRED AS EXTRAS FOR FILMING,

500 FRANCS, ONE DAY

NO EXPERIENCE NECESSARY

Without telling me, undoubtedly predicting my skepticism or flat refusal, M had sent my photo and the brief CV the producers requested, and now the voice speaking to me from the other end of the phone was explaining that I had been selected, and was slightly surprised to hear the apathy in my voice instead of the gratitude she was no doubt used to. And that was maybe why she asked me if I knew what film it was for. "It doesn't really matter," I told her, "I'm not an actor, I've never acted, I don't know how to be in front of a camera."

"Oh, but it's not just anyone's camera," she told me. "It's Polanski's. It's Roman Polanski's latest film."

That, of course, changed everything. On Saturday I spent a couple of hours going through secondhand places and my local video shop on Place Maubert, and that evening I rewatched *Rosemary's Baby*, and *Frantic*, and also *Death and the Maiden*, and at the same time as I felt again the same admiration and surprise as ever, what had happened to me so many times happened again: the inability to forget the disturbing relationship that was always there between the horror of the films and the horror of life, Polanski's afflicted life. But I soon forgot all of it except for one concrete fact: with a little luck, I was going to see him. I was going to see Polanski, would see him work. As I write these words today, when we all know so much more about Polanski, when the nasty details have emerged about another side of his life (which was unavailable to me back then, before the accusations and the arrest in Zurich), I have to wonder how my perception of his own suffering would have been different, what image I would have built about him in my head if I had also known the distress he had inflicted on others. Few people knew; I certainly didn't know. And on Sunday, at quarter to seven, I found myself there, in front of the café, along with a group of twenty or thirty people who were lined up, as I was, to sign a sort of agreement that included, among other clauses, an express ban on revealing details of the plot. The clause was useless, of course, because no aspect of the plot would be revealed to the extras, but we didn't know that when we signed. Nevertheless, the questions circulated among us: "What's it about?" "Who's in it?" "What do we have to do?" Names and rumors flew around, and we men and women of Mediterranean appearance formed a line and received pertinent instructions in the cool morning air, some of us in shirtsleeves, others barely protected by a light jacket, and soon boarded the bus that less than an hour later was pulling into a hidden parking lot at Charles de Gaulle Airport, a place closed to the public, where every thirty seconds you could hear a plane taking off (the escalating roar of engines) but where there was a noticeable absence of another noise: that of people. That's how those public spaces are when the public is absent. As I entered, though, I was not thinking about that, I don't think I was thinking about that. I was thinking about August 8, 1969, and I suspect I was not the only one.

The events of that night ended the decade of the sixties once and for all, it seems to me, and the proof is that I, who was born almost four years later, feel as if I'd been alive at that moment, as if I'd been one of the thousands of newspaper readers who gradually found out about the investigations and the results. As I have been able to verify over time, we all remember things differently, we all conserve our own chronology and even our own explanation of what happened. When I think about that night, I remember the strange configuration of the city of Los Angeles, full of niches in the hills that surround it, full of dead-end streets that skirt the hills. Cielo Drive is one of those streets, and number 10050 is the last house, where the street ends and turns back on itself. The house was long and set back more than a hundred yards from the gate; in fact, its position on the plot of land, as well as the generous foliage of the trees, kept it separate from the rest of the houses in the neighborhood. People arrived at the house through an electronic gate: there was a button on each side that allowed it to be opened without getting out of the car. But maybe the most important of all these details is that I do not know them firsthand, because, although I have been to Los Angeles, I've never been to Cielo Drive. There in Charles de Gaulle Airport, while getting ready to be an extra in a Polanski film, I realized I could describe the house and the trees and the entrance and the button that opened it because I'd seen photos, thousands of photos that began to appear in the press after that terrible night and that the following generations have inherited, more or less as we've inherited Zapruder's film—Kennedy's head exploding—or some of the photographs from Auschwitz, say, or Treblinka. And it's due to those photos, that unfortunate media memory, that any of us, the extras, could imagine the arrival of the murderers, shortly before midnight, at Polanski's house.

It seems they didn't use the gate out of fear that it was electrified: they entered by scaling a retaining wall. During the previous three days Los Angeles had been enduring a heat wave, and that same heat was in Charles de Gaulle Airport twenty-nine years later, while the extras were waiting in front of some glass doors for someone to open them for us. Or maybe that was just my impression? Polanski, who by 1969 was already a celebrity, had married an actress the year before who was far from fame, but was on her way: Sharon Tate. The photos, the television series, the film that came out that same year, all the images show a very beautiful woman, but they don't tend to remember that she was also an intelligent and daring woman, capable of moving in with Polanski in London shortly after meeting him, and able to see herself ironically after playing a particularly stupid part in a particularly stupid movie. But the truth is they were in love; their wedding, in January 1968, had caught the attention of the press, especially after the nude photos that *Playboy* had published and which had been taken by—that's right—Polanski. At the end of that year, Sharon Tate was pregnant: she was pregnant in February 1969, when the Polanskis decided to move from London to Los Angeles, taking up residence in the Cielo Drive house; she was pregnant during the whole first half of the year, while working on various projects in Europe; she was pregnant in July, when she boarded the *QE2*, alone, and traveled to Los Angeles. They had agreed that Polanski would arrive on August 12, a couple of weeks before the baby was due. On the 8th, Sharon Tate took a photo of herself in profile: the light is magnificent, and Tate appears with her hair up, in a swimsuit and T-shirt, flaunting her pregnancy. That night she went out for dinner with three friends: Jay Sebring, Abigail Folger, and Voytek Frykowski. They returned to the house on Cielo Drive at ten thirty, and Sharon Tate asked her friends to stay the night, so she wouldn't be on her own in her condition. A little while later, the four murderers—a man and three women, none of them older than twenty-three—arrived at the property in an old Ford, all dressed in dark clothing, all armed with knives, and one of them with a pistol. They climbed up one side of the hill, the man cut the telephone cables, and then they went back down to the gate. They scaled the retaining wall, and once inside they ran into the lights of a Rambler on its way out. The one who had cut the telephone cables told the girls to wait. He approached the Rambler, ordered it to stop, and shot the driver several times. The four began to walk toward the house. One of the women stayed outside. The rest looked for a way in.

I have spent short spells inside empty stadiums, inside museums after they'd closed, but I've never again felt the amazement I felt going inside Charles de Gaulle with a group of thirty people, made small and quiet as when we enter a cathedral (I say amazement, but I could also have said unease: it was unease produced by those high ceilings, cold floors, and windows everywhere). By that point we already knew that the title of the film was *The Ninth Gate*, that the plot was based on a Pérez-Reverte novel, *The Club Dumas*, and that the protagonists were played by Johnny Depp and Emmanuelle Seigner, Polanski's wife. "His third," someone corrected in French, and turning around I ran into a guy who could not have been over twenty-five and was already regretting his comment: Polanski's wives were, as everyone knew, a sensitive, even forbidden, subject. A young woman in a blue vest that identified her as part of the crew led us, through some passport inspection booths where there were neither officials nor passports to inspect, to a corridor brightly illuminated by daylight. Another group of extras joined ours; the young woman in the vest, along with a couple of colleagues, began to spread us out in the corridor, and that wing of the airport, which until that instant had seemed like a ghost town, a pretend Charles de Gaulle, slowly, mysteriously, began to come to life. And then, in the midst of the movement of people, of the extras' questions and the producers' answers that filled the air, the group opened and at the back, as still as an abandoned handcart on a siding, there was a black mobile platform with rubber wheels; on the platform, a camera, also black, and beside the camera a monitor, both machines covered in slight silvery glints (the discreet life of chrome and glass); and sitting in front of the camera, his arms so thin the sleeves of his T-shirt seemed to float around his biceps, was Polanski.

He was talking to another man, taller and heftier, who nodded submissively; both men's hands took turns moving toward the monitor and pointing at something, and then they went back to debating (the man looked at Polanski; Polanski, however, did not look at him). I observed him carefully, all the time thinking about scenes from his films, rooftops of Paris, car chases through New York's Chinatown, honeymoons on boats, making a conscious effort not to think about Cielo Drive and the events of 1969, as if doing so would be violating something, disrespecting something that deserved my respect (and maybe that was true). Meanwhile, we extras were receiving the description of the scene and our participation in it. Johnny Depp—the character Johnny Depp was playing—was arriving by plane in Madrid, he disembarked and started walking along with the other passengers, and only then did I look up and notice that the signs and posters of Charles de Gaulle Airport had been covered by signs and posters in Spanish or, to be precise, in Spanish and English: by virtue of the magic or the tricks of cinematic fiction, we were in Barajas airport. Later I would find out that Johnny Depp was on the trail of a book called *The Nine Gates to the Kingdom of Shadows*, that the book contained a series of engravings the correct interpretation of which could invoke the devil, and that crimes had already been committed that imitated the crimes in the engravings. But there, in the airport, I didn't know this yet. I learned about all that later; I had to wait to receive this information, yes, just as I had to wait to learn about Polanski's own transgressions. Ten years had to pass, give or take a few months, before the scandal broke out and our story (that story we build in our head about somebody else's life) was irreparably changed, and we had to go through the effort of rewriting somebody else's life. But that, as I say, would happen later.

Each of us had a particular choreography around Depp's

character, some walked beside him, others faster, beside the window, and one, only one, crossing between the actor and the camera. I'll never know why the producers decided that role should be mine, but I didn't have time to wonder about it for too long, because in a matter of seconds a barely perceptible commotion began and then the man who was beside Polanski stood up on the mobile platform and, while Polanski ducked down as if hiding behind the eye of the camera, shouted, almost with boredom or disdain, that word that more than an order is now a cliché: "Action!" We began to move according to the instructions, and the first time my attention could only concentrate on the routine, the way I had to walk, passing several other passengers without bumping into them, without even touching them, and I got within a few steps of Johnny Depp when someone (I didn't see who) shouted that other cliché "Cut!" and we extras continued to move for a second or two, like toys carrying on through inertia, till we stopped. While Polanski argued with his deputies, the people in the blue vests brought us back to our original positions. And it all started again: again Johnny Depp was arriving in Madrid, again on his face could be seen his grief over a friend's death. I didn't know that then either, but we extras would find out later, when we saw the movie. I remember precisely when I saw it: it was the following year, at a theater in Brussels. I also remember the compassion I felt for Johnny Depp when I saw the airport scene, and now I wonder if what I was feeling wasn't compassion for Polanski, and admiration as well, the inevitable admiration I always feel for survivors (but we didn't know back then how he had made others survivors as well, how others in the world had survived him). But maybe what I was feeling was that strange sensation, so very contemporary, that sort of code of our time besieged by images and violence, or by the violence of images: the sensation, derived from uncertainty, that everything could be fiction or, which is worse, that everything could be true. The sensation that there is no threat from the invented world that cannot pass into the real world and make us its victim. The sensation, in short, of the most primitive and infantile fear: the fear of credulity. If that was really what I was feeling, maybe the emotion came along with another I've never known what to call, but which appeared during that afternoon each time I looked at Johnny Depp and his pretend pain; for in front of him was another man whose face showed no pain, another man who was perhaps forcing himself at that very instant to pretend the opposite: serenity, resignation, maybe even oblivion.

I'll tell it as I remember it from the articles I've read and images I've seen, even though I wish I hadn't read or seen any of this. I am not the first nor will I be the last to reproduce what happened. I can tell it like this because time has gone by and the confusions and misunderstandings and the versions that existed in 1969, when for a long time they didn't know who the murderers were and why they had murdered, no longer exist for us. Three of them entered the house through the dining room window, and first came upon Voytek Frykowski, who was asleep on a sofa in the living room. "Who are you and what are you doing here?" The man answered: "I am the devil." The women walked around the house to see how many people were there: they found Abigail Folger in one bedroom and, in the other, Sharon Tate and Jay Sebring (each one of those who were going to die must have thought at that moment that the murderers were acquaintances, because all kinds of different people had always wandered through that house unannounced). In a few minutes they had all come back to the living room; the murderers ordered them to lie facedown on the floor; Sebring, pointing at Tate, asked that they allow her to sit, since she was pregnant, and the man's only reply was to shoot him. Then one of the women tied a rope around Sebring's neck and, with the other end of it around Sharon Tate's neck and Abigail Folger's neck, threw the rope over a beam and began to pull on it. One of the women jumped on Frykowski, who defended himself the best he could and in the struggle was stabbed several times; he ran out of the house, but the male murderer caught up to him and hit him with the butt of the revolver several times and then kicked him in the head. The other woman, meanwhile, over and over again stabbed Abigail Folger, who also managed to get outside and who would be found, wearing only a nightgown, on the manicured lawn. Sharon Tate was stabbed sixteen times. She pleaded with her murderer to let her go, to let her live, to allow her to have her baby. But her entreaties were in vain. Sharon Tate, Polanski's wife, died lying in the fetal position beside the sofa. The woman who killed her got a towel and used it to write, in her victim's blood on the bottom of the front door, a single word: *PIG*. Then she threw the towel away and it ended up landing on Jay Sebring's head; seeing the scene hours later, someone spoke of a sort of hood, and that gave rise to the infinite speculations about satanic sects that surrounded the investigation into the case during the following months. (Polanski had directed *Rosemary's Baby*, and that did nothing but increase the rumors; photos began to circulate of Sharon Tate practicing some macabre ritual, but someone pointed out that they were stills from *Eye of the Devil*, a film with an occultist plot in which Tate had starred in 1967.) Later, the two women and the man left through the gate to the property; the remaining woman was waiting for them in the Ford. They changed their clothes as they drove away through the canyon roads, threw the bloody clothes away in some wasteland, and around two in the morning they arrived back at the Spahn Ranch, where the leader of what they called "the Family" was waiting for them: Charles Manson. A small, skinny man, with long hair and a beard, who would later carve a cross between his eyebrows and then turn that cross into a swastika, a resentful failed composer who had been inspired by a Beatles song, "Helter Skelter," to order a series of crimes with no apparent motive, without any coherence, no trait in common apart from extreme cruelty, with the hope that they would be attributed to black people and provoke a race war. Manson, who had been in and out of prison since childhood, had two aliases registered in his criminal record: Jesus Christ and God.

We went through the airport scene seven times; seven times something came out wrong, or Polanski changed his mind, or a fault of the light forced him to correct the take. With each repetition the routine became more automatic, and my attention was left free to focus on other things, on Johnny Depp's jacket, on his beard that wasn't artificial but looked like it was, on the expression of studied disenchantment he assumed as he walked. After a certain moment I focused on the mobile platform and the fragile little man who was responsible for the nonexistent world we were all living in, the extras and Johnny Depp, the apocryphal world where Charles de Gaulle Airport had lost its identity and turned into Barajas. I was not a writer just starting out who was living in Paris and getting fed up with life in Paris and in a few months would move to Belgium and in a year would be arriving in Barcelona, but rather a passenger from a flight landing in Madrid who doesn't know that the man he's crossing paths with is about to come

into contact with a satanic sect. All of us, young people between twenty-five and thirty of Mediterranean appearance,
were other persons in a parallel world, all living at that moment on the orders of Roman Polanski, lord and master of our
lives and of their laws. Polanski had power over our move-
ments, he could order us to speak if he desired, he could control what we did in this parallel world and, most important,
he could control what others did to us. Had I known at that
moment all that I know today, had all the news reached me
and forced me to change my story, I would have seen that
power differently, maybe even realized the kind of damage it
can cause to someone vulnerable. But I didn't know. I tried to
imagine what Polanski felt in that world where everything
bad was rigorously watched over, like the explosion of a suspicious suitcase by an antiterrorist squad. I tried to put myself in
Polanski's place, I reached for all the empathy of which I'm
capable, and in the end I failed. There, in the French airport
transformed into a Spanish airport, I recognized the immense
distance that separated me from the man behind the camera;
I established, to put it like that, the limits of our imagination
and of our solidarity. Cut, someone said then, and the world
stopped again.

That evening, the same bus that had brought us that morning
dropped us off in the same place it had picked us up, in front

of the same closed café, and from there I arrived, after changing trains twice on the Métro, at my apartment on Rue Guy de la Brosse. I arrived so tired—it must have been the tension, I remember having thought, the terrible responsibility you feel, though in reality you don't have any, when you participate in a collective effort—that I could barely stop outside the Jussieu Métro station exit, at a Vietnamese street stall, to buy some takeout. But I didn't get as far as eating it: back in my apartment, I decided to lie down for a minute to recover before serving the food on a proper plate, and I ended up falling sound asleep and waking up three hours later, when the night was black and the silence, in that hidden little street, was almost total. My head ached: a dull pain behind my eyes made of blood that beats in the temples like a hangover. The apartment, of course, was in semidarkness, lit only by the weak yellow light from the streetlamps outside. That vague glow, coming in through the glass doors that opened onto the tiny balcony, made rectangles on the ceiling, or maybe they weren't rectangles, but trapeziums or rhomboids, figures that moved like searchlight beams looking for a fugitive, and that was the first thing I saw when I opened my eyes. It took me a fleeting instant to remember where I was—in a city that wasn't mine—and with whom—alone—and there was, in that instant of confusion, the urgency to speak with one voice among all the voices. *A beloved voice*: words from an old line of poetry, a line by a Colombian poet who did not write it to attenuate a moment of solitude. I lifted the receiver and dialed Belgium, where M was living, and the unease faded and became manageable only when she, finally, picked up the phone and told me that she was fine, that she'd had a good day, that no, nothing had happened to her. She was living in a big house in the middle of the Ardennes, a house surrounded by forests, whose owner hunted wild boar that his wife cooked, a stone house in which I would end up living for a while later. She asked me how the Polanski thing had gone and I said fine. "Only fine?" she asked. "Only fine," I said. But I added: "I don't want to talk about it." Then she must have heard something in my voice, must have understood something even before I understood it myself, or perhaps she understood it in a better way or a sharper or more generous or more discerning way, as she tends to understand things to my envy and amazement, because the conversation soon took another tack and M started to tell me that the noises I could hear were those of the wind blowing, and that outside, in the grove of trees that surrounded the house in the Ardennes, it was completely dark, but that she liked that darkness, and at the moment I called she had been playing with turning off the light in her room, on the third floor of the house, and looking out the window: if you let enough time go by, even here, in this perfectly dark night, the sky began to separate gradually from the land and the silhouettes of the very tall pines began to appear against that background, and if a gust of wind howled by, it was possible to see how the treetops swayed, from one side of the night sky to the other, resembling a group of strangers who look at us from the darkness, who look at us and howl at us and tell us no.

THE BOYS

They began to meet, who knows why, always as dusk was falling, always beside the wall that separated the green space from the avenue. They left their bicycles lying on the grass, or leaning against the wall like horses at a drinking trough, and then the fights started. There were never volunteers, but the rules were clear though never stated in words, and only once, with the circle already set up, was it necessary for the group to choose the boys—that the names had to be pronounced and their owners shamed—for them to begin to fight. The fights ended when one of the two gave in or when it got so dark that it was impossible to hit properly, but only one of the contenders could make the decision, no matter how much blood there was on their faces and clothes, no matter the tears, no matter the crunch of bone against bone. What happened afterward was up to each one of them: the boys went home with a broken nose or the skin scraped off their cheeks by the blows, and gave the best explanations they could or got by without giving any, sneaking in without being seen and getting into the shower and then turning off the light without saying good night, confident their parents would put it all down to the difficulties of adolescence, the anarchy of new hormones.

The neighborhood had once been a street like any other, a series of different houses built randomly as if someone had dropped them from the sky. But one day they decided to put a gatehouse at each end, there where the sinuous street met other bigger or more important or at least straighter ones, and the public thoroughfare became a closed complex: a meandering place where people could have the normal life that before—before these difficult times—had been possible in the city. At the gatehouses, the security guards raised the thick aluminum barriers, with diagonal yellow and black stripes, and then the authorized or known cars entered the neighborhood and arrived slowly at their houses, past children having a kick-about with deflated balls and skateboards that could be left outside in the relative confidence that they'd still be there the next morning. The green spaces were nooks and crannies that had formed between the houses, and some of them, like the corner where the fights took place, were out of the adults' sight, in the neighborhood's blind spots, separated from the hostile city by a high concrete wall crowned with barbed wire. Nobody remembered whether the wall existed before the

gatehouses closed off the street. Maybe they'd been improvised, with the urgency of the pursued, to seal the neighborhood on the only flank that otherwise would have remained
open.

On the other side of the wall, behind where the fights took
place, there was a bakery that sold sweet *mojicón* buns and a
drugstore where the boys picked up the Sunday papers for
their fathers, and packets of clandestine cigarettes. Castro was
in charge of buying them and later handing them out. The
rest respected him for his age and size and also for being the
son of a judge, but most of all for the fact that the judge had
been murdered. They knew he'd been investigating the murder of the Minister of Justice, two years earlier, and that the
Cali drug dealers had been involved in the case, not just the
Medellín cartel, who were already starting to be on everyone's
lips. Then, one fine day, the judge began to see suspicious people around his house and on his way out of the courts; but he
refused to have official protection, arguing that he didn't want
the hit men to kill anyone else when trying to kill him. In July
(it was a Tuesday) he got into a taxi on the Avenida de las
Américas and asked the driver to take him to Calle 48. When
he arrived at his destination, a green Mazda pulled up behind
the taxi, and a man with a scarf tied around his face got out of
the Mazda. Without a question, without a threat, without an
insult, the man with the scarf shot the judge nine times at point-
blank range. His wife, who was waiting for him in a nearby

funeral home, for an acquaintance's wake, found out only when the coroner's office was taking the body away.

They saw Castro cry that night, when his mother came looking for him at the wooden benches where the boys were talking about sex, but never again. That Friday he came to fight, and they all agreed that his fury was understandable but that he should have stopped when the other asked for mercy, with one eye already shut from the blows and his lips swollen and teeth all clearly outlined by the blood running down from his gums. Maybe Castro was ashamed later, because he stayed away from the group for several weeks, not showing up by the brick wall, and the boys mentioned the fact but didn't do anything about it: didn't wait at the door of his house, or look for him at the drugstore, or ask his mother, now dressed in black and suddenly older. In the end, when the evenings recovered their lost normality, nobody mentioned the murdered judge: it was as if the crime had never happened, or as if it had happened to somebody else, in another country, far from the neighborhood and the wall and six in the evening. The other, the one who fought Castro that day, never came back. And the boys forgot him effortlessly, almost without noticing. When his family moved to another neighborhood, nobody went to say goodbye, and nobody remembers him saying goodbye to any of them.

One day when Castro, for whatever reason, wasn't there, it

occurred to one of the boys to do something that would not have been possible in his presence.

"Tomorrow," he said, "let's go see the place where they killed the captain."

They met an hour earlier: sneaking out of the neighborhood was a worrying transgression, but doing it at nightfall was running incalculable risks. They found a place on the wall where the barbed wire had loosened over the years, gradually, leaving a space a skillful body could slip through; leaning the tallest bicycle against the wall, a heavy-framed Monark with a seat that could be raised a whole hand's height, the boys scaled the wall one by one, and there were ripped clothes and sore hands, but all of them eventually jumped down to the sidewalk of the major avenue. Pinzón, who'd had the idea, directed them along the broken paving stones, they passed in front of the bakery and past the drugstore and past the tree where a man with swollen eyes had once offered one of them a paper twist of cocaine, and in a matter of eleven blocks, after crossing the canal with its scant and smelly water, arrived at the street where the crime had occurred.

"It was here," Pinzón said.

That was where it was. There, on that very sidewalk where the boys now looked toward the noisy traffic, the hit man had stood waiting for his victim. Two months had gone by since then. The hit man was eighteen, just four or five years older than the boys, and had arrived that same morning—on the back of a motorbike—from some tropical village where he already had a death on his hands. They'd paid him a hundred thousand pesos to kill Captain Rodríguez, of the anti-narcotics squad, and everything seemed to indicate that it had been easier than expected, because the captain had left his house without bodyguards in spite of his life having been publicly threatened. The hit man described it all to the police during the following days, but at a certain moment he changed his story. As coldly as he'd told the previous version, he told them he'd arrived in Bogotá by bus, that he'd fallen asleep on the way there and got out of the bus when he woke up, and had the bad luck to be right in the middle of the attack. He said he'd been frightened by the gunshots and that was why he'd run. He said that was why, because he'd been running, the police had arrested him. He said the police had tortured a confession out of him, and showed the bruises left on his body from the torture. He said he didn't know who Captain Rodríguez was or why he had been killed.

"And who can prove," Pinzón said, "that he wasn't telling the truth."

The boys were disappointed that no trace remained of the violence: no stain, no bullet hole in any nearby wall. And then, as if Pinzón felt responsible for something, as if he felt he'd let the group down, in a matter of seconds he was taking them even farther, farther away from the neighborhood. "Where are we going?" someone asked, but Pinzón was walking at a leader's pace and crossing streets without too much care and the smaller ones were having a hard time keeping up. When they arrived, Pinzón stopped proudly beside a bust mounted on a shiny pedestal. The boys recognized in the bronze face the features of the Minister of Justice. They had hunted him down very close to here; just there, at the tight curve, the murderers' motorbike had skidded as they tried to escape the bodyguards, and the boys remembered the images of the hit man injured in the fall, crying like a child at the moment he was captured. Pinzón, standing beside the statue with its empty eyes and hard features, looked at the rest of them as if someone had to take his photo.

They were back in their neighborhood before night fell, with enough time to get home without rousing any suspicions, but then they realized they didn't have a bicycle to scale the wall where they'd come out. Lifting the lightest on their shoulders, they could get him high enough to reach the top, but someone would be left below; so they decided to arrive all together in a pack at the north-end gatehouse, where the security guard, Carrasco, intimidated them less than the other—a certain feebleness in his voice, a certain fear in his eyes—and try to enter as if nothing unusual had happened. The security guards were bored men in shit-colored uniforms, with flashlights and pistols on their belts; the fights very soon stopped mattering to them, and they even watched them from a distance sometimes, hands behind their backs and empty expressions under their caps, and they disappeared under the streetlights as soon as a winner began to gain ground. However, this, letting the boys out without permission, could not be ignored. Carrasco lifted the intercom receiver, but before he could call any house, Pinzón was handing him a two-thousand-peso note.

"You look better when you're quiet, Carrasco," he said. "Hang up and don't stick your nose into things that don't concern you."

Pinzón knew more than the others because his father was a detective. In their circle, the word evoked long trench coats and dark glasses, and Pinzón had had to explain that no, his father was a normal, regular person and rather boring, who went every day to a very tall building on the other side of the city, and had an office there beside other offices of other employees who dressed the same and were just as boring, in spite of the fact that their job put them in daily contact with the most-wanted criminals in the country. Pinzón's father was a shy little man who'd never been seen with a woman: he had arrived in the neighborhood without a wife, with his motherless son in tow, and his solitude was so notorious that insidious rumors were soon circulating around the neighborhood: that Pinzón was the accidental son of a secretary, it was sometimes said, and also that his father actually liked men. The truth, which was eventually discovered, was that Pinzón's mother had died of some drawn-out illness, and moving to the neighborhood—beginning a new life in another house with new people—had been his father's only way of fighting his grief. The boys had a hard time reconciling that man with the sparse mustache, knitted tie, and argyle sweater with the risks of bugging the telephones of a drug trafficker or a corrupt police officer, or with the privilege of designing the security strategy for a threatened politician. They never saw him leave for work, but they saw him return in his Renault 6 with its fragile bodywork and halfhearted horn and enter his house with his head down between his shoulders as if forever in a cold wind. And they imagined him telling Pinzón the things he'd seen or learned at work, the secrets of the outside world, the news that would come out the next day in the papers. Or that would maybe never come out, that was also possible.

At the end of October they killed another magistrate. A magistrate, the boys knew, was a judge like Castro's father, but more important. The dead man had issued an arrest warrant for Pablo Escobar, accusing him of old crimes that nobody remembered anymore, and funeral wreaths immediately began to arrive at his house with pale flowers and his name written in golden letters on a purple sash. The magistrate did not rescind the accusations, and that struck many as brave; but what nobody understood was what he did next, when the drug traffickers began to threaten his family as well. It was said that the magistrate's wife had been stopped at a military roadblock on a mountain road; the men in uniform ordered her out of the car, put it in neutral, and pushed it over the cliff.

"Next time," one of them told her, "we won't let you out."

They weren't army soldiers, but men who worked for the Medellín cartel. Later, when the wife became pregnant, Escobar found out and let the magistrate know that he would kill her and the baby if he didn't retract the accusations; the magistrate replied, refusing to retract anything, but promising him a fair trial. And that day, the day of the crime, the magistrate and his wife were driving down an avenue in Medellín when a white pickup truck blocked their way. Three men got out, walked up to the window through which the judge was watching them, and began to fire. The magistrate died at the scene, lying on the pavement. His wife, incredibly, survived two bullet wounds without even losing consciousness.

For several weeks, Pinzón took an interest in the survivor and tried to find out what had happened to the baby, if it was a boy or a girl, if it was all right even though it was going to be born without a father. When he heard of the birth, he wrote the little boy (who was named Ángel) a short note: *Welcome to this shitty country*. He gave it to his father and asked him to send it to the widow. His father tore it up in front of him, but that was not as surprising as the violent slap he delivered next, which achieved what the punches by the wall never had: a few brief tears, more like the slimy trail of a snail, slid down Pinzón's red cheek.

At the end of the following year, shortly before the first bombs exploded, the boys began to leave the neighborhood, sometimes with their parents' permission and sometimes in the face of their helplessness, to gather on the back steps of the mall, beside the parking lot. There were twenty brick steps by which you could enter the second floor of the gigantic building to go to the part where the video games were, a dark space with neon lights where the electric noises forced them to shout to one another and where the air was stale with the foul smoke their new lungs exhaled. But they also liked the stairs because from them they could control the eastern edge of the parking lot, where the other groups liked to arrive. And it didn't matter whether the encounter took place on the steps or inside the arcade or outside the door of the pizzeria: the fights were arranged and then it was just a matter of crossing the canal to an open space or setting up the huddle in one corner of the parking lot, for nobody ever went there, and the fight would be over before the security guards noticed it. They were different from the ones in the neighborhood, because these guards didn't know the boys or owe their meager salaries to their parents, and didn't think twice about dispersing the groups with ferocious truncheon blows capable of breaking bones and bruising flesh.

There, in the parking lot, with other boys from other parts of the immense city, the rules were different. Nobody knows who was the first to bring a bicycle chain, and it's almost certain the idea did not come from their neighborhood; but the important thing is that those from the neighborhood imitated them very quickly, since the only thing forbidden was not defending yourself, or rather, the only right was the right not to be outdone. A blow from a chain was fearful because it cut the skin like a swipe from a claw and also because the wound would often get infected, perhaps from the oil or the rust, and then hiding the incidents (or the ointments, or antibiotics) would be more difficult. That was what happened to Castro, who one weekend, just after the Christmas holidays, ended up confronting a guy with a shaved head whose nickname, Clash, stopped being funny very quickly. Castro arrived back in the neighborhood with his school shirt ripped by the chain; in a matter of hours the adults had all gathered at his house, in Judge Castro's living room, and there were concerns and indignant voices and conversations with the boys at dining room tables, and Castro's mother stopped saying hello the way she used to greet them before.

"If I have to bury this one too," she said to them all furiously, "it'll be your fault."

Castro's mother, the judge's widow, was a tall, thin woman

who wore turtleneck sweaters and tartan kilts, on whose flat chest hung a pair of plastic-framed glasses. Her name was Susana (she introduced herself with her husband's surname, Susana de Castro), and she had taken the reins of her house with a firm hand, but everyone was surprised that she also took on the leadership of the neighborhood, creating committees and lecturing the other parents and setting up regular meetings to talk about drugs and vandalism and shirts torn by bicycle chains. Nothing changed in the neighborhood, in any case, for the inertia of violence is like a deep underground current that nobody can reach; or, to put it a better way, something did change, but not how the neighborhood expected. Looking back on it years later, it's easy to understand how it happened the way it did (hard times bring victims together), or it's difficult to justify the general surprise, the gossip among adults in the houses, the net curtains pulled back a little when Susana de Castro crossed the street to ring the doorbell of Pinzón's father's house, or when Pinzón's father started up his Renault 6 at seven in the evening and picked her up twenty steps down the street and drove out the northern gate with her to return three hours later and drop her off at her house like a teenager, like a Cinderella who had just defied the risks of going out at night in the unsociable city.

It's just that nobody went out, or only those who had nothing to lose did. In those days, a mafioso had gone into a nightclub in the mountains with his private army, had closed it by virtue of his machine guns, and had taken away two women that he fancied (and one of the husbands, who tried to object, got three bullets in the chest). In March, a politician was murdered in the Bogotá airport, and in the shoot-out others were wounded who weren't even in the murderers' plans; in July the drug traffickers wanted to kill a police colonel, but the bomb they set off ended up killing six people (and none of them was the police colonel); the next day, a squad of soldiers at the service of the drug traffickers forced their way into a building in the north end of the city and murdered four intelligence agents who were working, it seems, on an anti-narcotics operation. This happened forty blocks from Castro's house, where Pinzón's father was eating chicken with rice in front of Doña Susana and her son, smiling and laughing and talking about his work, coming out with various anecdotes to impress the woman and also the boy: protected witnesses, clandestine operations, DEA informants who were discovered and murdered.

The boys wondered what was happening there (it was a vague *there*, an imprecise and conveniently ambiguous *there*), but nobody dared to mention the matter in Castro's or Pinzón's presence, nobody was ready to light a fuse with unpredictable consequences. Then, in August, Doña Susana and Pinzón's father were seen going out together one night, their silhouettes in plain sight through the back window of the Renault 6. It should have been a night like previous nights, a routine in which the Renault 6 comes back later with the same couple inside it and stops first in front of one house for a woman to get out, and there are *good night*s through the open car window, or maybe the man gets out and walks her to her door and pretends not to notice her son watching from the second floor. Yes, that's how it should have happened.

But it didn't happen like that. That night was different, because on the other side of the city, before beginning to speak on a wooden platform in front of an audience of his followers, a presidential candidate was gunned down by drug traffickers' hit men. It was a special crime, not just due to the affection people had for the slain man, but also because the tragedy was recorded forever by the cameras that were going to cover the event, so everyone in the city saw the well-dressed body fall with a dry thud on the wood (and they would continue to see it) and everyone heard the bursts of machine-gun fire and the screams and the crying and the desperation (and they would continue to hear it). And it was different for the neighborhood, and for the boys of the neighborhood, because the curfew that was immediately declared caught Doña Susana and Pinzón's father far from their homes. The streets were deserted in minutes; the police occupied them, the army occupied them, and one of those silences that sound like something about to break fell over the city. It was a long night, a night of lit-up windows and insomnia in the bedrooms and boys who, in the accidental or unexpected solitude of their houses, masturbated with the door open.

Doña Susana and Pinzón's father did not return to the neighborhood that night. No one ever found out where they were when the curfew was announced: a restaurant, someone's house? But the next morning, when they finally appeared, it was as if they were two different people. Pinzón's father was smiling; and that smile—and the way Doña Susana fixed her hair so the August wind wouldn't mess it up—was on everyone's lips for days.

On the neighborhood's windows, crosses of white tape began to appear: someone had said that it was the only way to prevent a nearby bomb blast from turning the glass into murderous shards. For the boys, the neighborhood began to look like a gigantic map where there was a treasure in each house, for in each window shone a white X, and one night someone decided to test the strategy. It was late and nobody saw those who went by, flashes of bicycles, throwing fist-sized stones; the glass broke in only two houses, because the boys' aim was not so good or their arms weren't strong enough, but everyone saw how the broken windows fell in four big pieces. They tried to find the guilty parties, but to no avail.

That was how the neighborhood was, crisscrossed with masking tape, the December morning that Pinzón's father invited Doña Susana to see the Christmas decorations at his office. It seemed they'd been working on them for days, putting

up decorated trees on every floor, painting angels and shooting stars on windows, stringing up lights wherever possible
and even buying real moss for a life-sized nativity scene they
were setting up in the director's office. The idea hadn't been
his, but that of a technician from Computer Programming.
His fiancée, from Criminology, agreed that the detectives
needed to relax, enjoy themselves, talk about other things, because the persecution of the drug cartels, which occupied their
days and nights, had not left them a free moment to feel the
Christmas spirit. So the couple (because that's what they were
by then, a couple) drove away from the neighborhood in the
Renault 6 at the same time the boys left for the avenue to wait
for their buses.

Of what happened there, on Calle 19, very little would be
known. It is most likely that Doña Susana and Pinzón's father
would not yet have entered the building at 7:32 a.m., when the
five hundred kilos of dynamite the drug traffickers' hit men
had loaded onto an Aqueducts and Sewers bus (that amount
of explosives would only fit on a bus) blew up. They said that
was the most likely scenario because there were more people
killed outside the building than in, more people crushed by
the facade that crashed onto the sidewalk—concrete boulders
raining down everywhere—than by the ceilings of the offices.
The Director of Intelligence, the main target of that act of
war, was not among the seventy dead, but a newspaper recy-
cler was and so was a woman who sold coffee from a little

aluminum cart. Later, a legend began to run through the neighborhood: that Doña Susana had fallen down with a shard of glass lodged in her leg, and that someone had seen Pinzón's father crouched beside her, and after removing the glass, taking off his tie to make her a tourniquet. But maybe it was only a legend, something a boy gets told to mitigate his pain or so the pain doesn't get mixed up with other pains (so he has something unique and worthy, something he can tell, something that rescues this death from the terrible anonymity of death), since neither of them survived the attack, and their bodies in their torn clothing were among the dozens the fire-fighters recovered from the rubble.

The final fight took place in the canal, in part because it had run dry or had just a tiny trickle of water running through it. They hadn't planned it that way, but the boys met in the parking lot of the mall and the matter was settled without much negotiation: they left through the eastern gate, maybe intending to cross the canal by the narrow bridge and find the fields that opened out five or six blocks farther along, and before anyone had noticed they were careening down the steep concrete sides, carried by the slope and the desire to hurt. It was difficult to form a huddle like the other times, because the sides were uneven and slippery, but somehow they managed to get close to the tunnel (one of those tunnels where one standing person fits) and construct the space where Choco and Pinzón, who'd had it in for each other for some time, could finally bash each other's faces in. They fought bare-knuckle, with no chains or knives, and maybe that was why Choco, who was a head taller and quite a few kilos heavier than Pinzón, began very quickly to gain a certain advantage. The boys would later talk about the traces of blood on the banks of the canal, some of them in the shape of a hand reaching out to keep from falling, and they would also talk about the shouts that echoed in the tunnel, the shouts of encouragement and also of hatred. But it was hard to get them to talk of the end, when Choco already had Pinzón on the ground and Pinzón was defending himself with his head in the dirty water, twisting like a dung beetle on its back. Castro approached slowly, so slowly that they didn't see him coming. The boys remembered having seen him sitting on the canal wall, his knees against his chest, and later, without any transition whatsoever, bursting into the center of the huddle (and violating the rules as he did) as if he wanted to examine the fight up close. Even Choco was disconcerted when he saw him coming, and he didn't really know what to do when Castro's first kick sank into the fallen boy's ribs and made him release a single faltering yell. Castro walked slowly around the fallen body and kicked him again, this time putting all his strength into the toe cap, as if to be sure of smashing his kidneys, and then, at the same time as the first appeals began to be heard, the first worried or terrified voices, he kicked him in the head, once, twice, and a patch of blood appeared in his ear and under his neck. Although maybe it wasn't blood, the boys would say, because later, when Pinzón stopped defending himself, his body stayed lying on the ground, the neck bathed by the dirty water, and it was possible, it was very possible, that it was mud that was staining it.

THE LAST CORRIDO

I accepted the commission because it paid well, but most of all because I had gotten the rather absurd notion into my head that a weeklong bus journey would finally prove to me whether Spain was a country in which I could live, or if I had made yet another mistake about my destiny, if I would have to pack my bags for a fourth time and find somewhere else to settle. The idea was to accompany a Mexican corrido band on their tour of the Iberian Peninsula, write an article about them, and publish it in Mexico, as part of a tribute to the band. So on July 17, 2001, I met with one of their representatives, a man with a colossal double chin and a shirt that was too small for him, received a laminated card that I could hang around my neck (there was my name, with a spelling mistake, and also my position: entourage), and that same night, shortly before nine, I arrived at the Razzmatazz club in Barcelona. On the poster at the entrance, beside the cage where a girl signaled with her hands that there were no tickets left, it said *The Márquez Brothers* and, underlined: *One Night Only.*

Outside the day was still bright. That was one of the worst summers—I'd been told—in recent years: inside, however, the world was black and the temperature fell brutally. And in that windowless hall with walls that absorbed light, where the air-conditioning did its best to neutralize or confuse the smell of human sweat, the concert had already begun. I leaned on the bar, at a prudent distance from the audience and their jumping and their Mexican flags the size of sheets, and waited. When the last corrido finished, a woman ran up on the stage, took off her bra, and gave it to the singer. The singer, a very young man with a sparse mustache but a fierce voice, took it, hung it carefully from a microphone (under the black lights the white of the lace turned an intense violet color), and disappeared behind the door to the dressing rooms. I followed him. I made my way through a group of bikers, saw the words *Hells Angels* on their backs and smelled belched beer on their breath; I wondered what a group like that could be doing at a concert like this, and as I advanced through a narrow hallway, badly lit by a single neon tube, I was received, or rather intercepted, by the same man who had given me the card. "Let them change their clothes," he said. "You don't want to catch them in their skivvies." At the back, behind a half-open door, were the musicians. I noticed they weren't looking at or talking to one another. They moved as if each of them were alone in front of the mirror, changing their shirts, running a comb through their hair. And what happened, happened later, once the whole audience had left.

The hall had been left covered in trampled cans and plastic glasses. On the bar, near the corner where I had been leaning when I first arrived, there was a cheap paper tablecloth and an arrangement of water jugs and fizzy drinks, sandwiches and tortillas wrapped in aluminum foil. While we ate, the agent (Alonso was his name) told me the band had gotten together in 1968, and that they were all brothers, except for Ricardo. I asked which one was Ricardo. "Ricardo is our new vocalist," Alonso said. "The first Márquez Brothers record is the same age as him. See him over there, he's the son of the one beside him." The one beside him was one of the musicians, the only one in the whole group who didn't have a mustache; I was told his name, but I didn't retain it at that moment. I saw them, I compared them, and it's true that they seemed the same age, not father and son. And then I asked an innocent question, a question with no other intention than merely to gain information, a question that—it seemed to me—came directly out of what we'd been talking about: "And who sang before?" And at that very moment one of the bikers arrived, forced a disposable camera into my hand, and went to stand beside the musicians. I took his photo and saw him pull out a wrinkled piece of paper to ask for their autographs; I listened to him explain, while he adjusted a wristband with metal studs on it, that he had first heard the band in San Francisco and that he had all their records, since the time of Ernesto.

"Who's Ernesto?" I asked.

"The oldest brother," Alonso said. "The one who started the group."

"And he's not here?"

"Their father was paralyzed in the sixties. Ernesto put the band together just to survive. Did you ask who used to sing? It was him. It was Ernesto. This group was his life."

"The greatest of all time," said the biker.

"Yes," Alonso said. "The greatest." He asked the biker to go, putting a hand on the emblem on his jacket and pushing him diplomatically, and then he said to me: "But now we're tired, now we're going to sleep."

We went out into the Barcelona night, the warm wind of eleven o'clock at night, and Alonso told me where I should be at ten o'clock the next morning to leave for Valencia. I walked home and, feeling strangely excited, poured myself a gin and tonic, opened all the windows, the ones overlooking the inner patio and the ones overlooking the square and its palm trees, and I began to read the press dossier. And I learned that five years earlier, the Márquez Brothers had toured Spain on an identical tour—same itinerary, same set list, and very similar dates—to the one they'd just started with me on board. Five years ago, the tour had also started in Barcelona; five years ago they'd also moved on to Valencia; five years ago they'd also played in three other cities, and had finished up in Cartagena, in the middle of an international music festival, which had then been transmitted live to all of Latin America, as would undoubtedly happen this time. The only difference between that past tour and this tour now was the presence of one man. I looked through the dossier for a photo of Ernesto Márquez, the founder of the band, the man who, after his father's paralysis, had recruited his brothers (amateur guitarists, weekend accordion players) to save the family from starvation. But I didn't find anything. The man wasn't there anymore, I thought. Ernesto Márquez, the missing one.

That afternoon in 1996, before the concert in Valencia, Ricardo Márquez was talking to the sound engineers, checking over the decks and speakers with them, when he saw Ernesto walking between the trees of the park on his own. The idea of a concert in the open air had been his, and so it was normal that Ernesto would want to walk around the stage, perhaps trying to anticipate where the gate-crashers would sneak in this time, there were always a few. But he didn't look attentive, he looked downcast; every once in a while he held a hand to his throat, and once Ricardo saw him raise his face, look up toward the treetops as if a leaf had just fallen on his graying hair, and he knew he was making an enormous effort to swallow. He recognized that gesture, because he'd seen him do it before (after the Barcelona concert, for example). He climbed down from the side of the stage, where the sound crew was; he thought they would need to light those steps better, to prevent anyone from getting tangled up in a wire and fucking up the whole show. It was already dark and in the whole park the crickets had burst out chirping almost simultaneously. Ricardo looked at his watch: the concert would start in a few hours, and Ernesto had started to gulp.

It was serious, for this tour wasn't just any tour: they were recording it for a live album, and a lot was riding on that album. It couldn't go wrong. There were many things Ricardo didn't understand, many matters of royalties and percentages of ticket sales and rented equipment, but he had understood this very well: that the live album of the Spanish tour had to come out well.

Ricardo arrived at the two trailers where the organizers had installed the dressing rooms and where at that time all the Márquez brothers, except Ernesto, were doing their warm-up exercises, all moving around their own rooms like caged animals, from one side to the other, and all with their ears covered by a pair of yellow headphones. They moved their heads, stuck out their tongues, shouted those exercises that Ricardo knew by heart, among other reasons because he could do them better than they could. He looked through the windows for his father, and gave the metal door of the trailer a couple of raps with his knuckles, and his father took off his headphones, irritated by the interruption. "I'm looking for Uncle Ernesto," he said.

"He's in his dressing room," his father said.

"He's not there."

"He must be in his dressing room. It's almost time."

His father left the Walkman on top of a plastic table and went out, and Ricardo saw he had already put on his concert outfit, blue leather trousers and jacket with sequins that shone when they passed under any spotlights. They walked to the corner of the trailers, where they could get a look over the park without being seen by the public, who had already started to fill up the ground, and Ricardo saw that his father was beginning to worry (his hands nervously rubbing the embroidered sides and epaulettes of his outfit) when his uncle Ernesto appeared.

"And what are you doing?" Ricardo's father said. "Aren't you warming up?"

Ernesto answered in a perfect eight-syllable line, like the ones he wrote in the corridos: "A rooster is always crowing."

Ricardo took a few steps back and saw them exchange three phrases he had memorized, his father asking if he felt all right and his uncle saying yes, why wouldn't he feel fine, and somehow protesting the scrutiny he'd been submitted to since the last concert. And then his father would say something like it wasn't *since the last concert* and then *it goes back further than that* and then *you've been like this for too long* and then *one day your throat will give out.* All that must have been said, because right there, standing in front of his brother, Ernesto put his headphones on and with a movement of one finger on the Walkman obliterated the whole world, the complaints, the worries, the threats. Ricardo's father was left talking to himself, looking at the effort that caused Ernesto (his vocal cords, his larynx) obvious discomfort, but discomfort that was not reflected in the quality of his voice, and was therefore of no use to anyone to prove anything. Ernesto Márquez stepped into his dressing room (the exercises no longer audible) and came back out only when it was time to go onstage.

Ricardo watched the concert from the wings. He liked to do that, and during open-air concerts he liked to climb down in the middle of a song and walk behind the stage, where the world, perhaps due to the violent contrast with the lights and the music, seemed unusually dark and secret, almost peaceful. He went from one wing to the other, and on the way he thought that his destiny was on the stage, in front of the microphone, in the space that the voice of Ernesto Márquez was filling right then. As a teenager, Ricardo had admired that throat which had supported the family and to which they all owed a debt of gratitude, but which gave the impression of beating a retreat. Everything was changing, everything was changing too quickly, and the situation the family lived in was transformed every hour. They'd received the diagnosis six months earlier. (Ricardo wasn't uncomfortable with this use of the plural, because they'd all received it, not just the one who was ill.) Actually, Ernesto's illness had begun earlier, but the doctors in Los Angeles all agreed that the cancer of the colon was not related to that of the larynx. In any case, the prognosis was not fatal, and there was a positive side to that whole situation: the cancer didn't affect Ernesto's voice or, to judge from the life he'd been leading since the diagnosis, his capacity for daily work. He went on writing songs and performing them in public, and he went on traveling on five- and seven- and nine-hour flights to accept the well-paid invitations from gangsters in Colombia or Mexico or from festivals in Buenos Aires or Santiago.

But that seemed to be changing. Was it changing? It seemed to be changing. From the wings Ricardo saw how Ernesto Márquez walked up to the third level of the stage and descended from there shrouded in artificial mist singing "Los Poderosos," despite someone having mentioned that inhaling that mist was not good for his throat. Ricardo thought he'd say something to him when the concert finished, because much more than the vocalist's prestige depended on that voice, and he, like any other Márquez, had a right to protect what was his.

So later, while the roadies packed up the equipment and the makeup artists put away the makeup, when the Márquez brothers had sat down to rest (to enjoy the cool night air outside the leather of those outfits that made them sweat like mules), Ricardo made an apparently casual comment about what he'd seen earlier. He didn't say it in so many words, but the image floating through the night was that of a gray-haired man with his hand at his throat and walking a little hunched over, perhaps from the weight of an accordion; a man who lifts his head to swallow without pain; a man who they all respect, of course, but who was putting the band's reputation at risk every day and with each concert the moment grew closer that his voice, if only from erosion over the years, from nodes or polyps or stubborn colds, fails in the middle of a concert the way power fails during a storm.

Ernesto Márquez didn't answer, but stood up and walked slowly around the plastic table. He got to where his nephew was and slapped him hard, and would have hit him again if his brothers hadn't grabbed his arms. And in the subsequent silence, in the gaze of the whole team, Ernesto Márquez raised his voice.

"I still have songs inside me," he said, and then turned to Ricardo. "And you, get it through your skull, you're going to have to do a lot more than that to take over my spot."

They all got on the bus.

During the long five hours of the trip from Valencia to Madrid I could not stop thinking for a moment that the bus I was traveling in was repeating or tracing, with certain tiny differences in the dates, the route that other bus had covered five years earlier. (With two particularities: one passenger from then was absent this time; a passenger who didn't exist then was now present.) It was our third day together, and my spontaneous and almost involuntary inquisitions of the first night in the Razzmatazz had not gotten me off on a good footing. The Márquez Brothers did not feel the slightest desire to facilitate my construction of the article, neither through their answers to my questions—which were frugal, forgetful, always more likely to close paths than open them—nor through the simpler act of their company, which they hid from me, afraid, no doubt, that I would end up asking them about Ernesto Márquez. When I managed to get one of them to talk to me they spoke of inanities; so I found out that Alonso had a dog called Chiquita, that he'd rescued her from the street, and he wouldn't think of crossbreeding her, because her body was too small and designed to have no more than two puppies. Alonso didn't want a larger dog to get her pregnant and for her to have problems giving birth. "One has to take care of little animals," he told me. "Or perhaps you've not heard 'Los Perros y los Niños'?" I told him no, I hadn't heard "The Dogs and the Children"; Alonso was not terribly surprised, and even tolerated somewhat patronizingly my asking him if he were talking about a corrido.

That evening, on the Madrid stage, the Márquez Brothers rehearsed in suits and ties despite the temperature never going lower than thirty degrees Celsius. They wore starched collars, double-breasted jackets, gold cuff links, and turned-up trousers that Hugo, the drummer, bound with masking tape so the cuffs wouldn't get tangled in the pedals (the same tape the musicians used to fix the set lists to the floor of the stage). And that time I had my first impression confirmed: watching them prepare for the night's concert on the black stage, it was impossible not to sense that there was a strange melancholy among them. When Ricardo and his father went over the lyrics on a laptop computer, Ricardo put a hand on his father's shoulder to steady himself in a crouch, or standing up after checking, a finger against the screen, a change in rhythm or a modified line; and those gestures, which in any other situation would have seemed intimate or affectionate, were contaminated there, and it was impossible not to notice.

It was also impossible not to notice that my article was failing with every minute I spent with the members of the band. Suddenly I found myself walking aimlessly through the concert venue, like a guest who was not welcome at a party. It was a sort of walled and cobbled courtyard, more suited to nineteenth-century firing squads than the Márquez Brothers' kitsch eight-syllable lines (their hymns to the immigrant, their stories of ill-fated love in Tijuana). Anyway, the musicians' dressing rooms were in a caravan almost leaning against the wall like a sad animal; on the opposite side of the courtyard, twenty or so yards away, some Mexicans had set up a cart of food brought, as they explained, directly from Guadalajara. It was a sort of stagecoach from which they were selling fizzy drinks, chips, tortillas, and Corona beer. On the cart was a sign that I bent down to get a better look at:

> *The guy who gives credit isn't here*
> *He went to smash in the face*
> *of someone who owed him*

That was what I was doing when Ricardo Márquez came up beside me. He had changed his clothes. He was wearing a blue leather suit, and a pair of headphones around his neck like a collar. I stood up, said hello, saw him ask for a bottle of water, he, who had three whole liters in his dressing room at any hour of the day. I imagined that what interested him at that moment was not the bottle of water. "Was it like this five years ago too?" I asked. "Was this little cart here?"

Ricardo smiled. "No, this little cart wasn't here."

"And the rest?"

"The rest is exactly the same," Ricardo said. "You're Colombian, aren't you?"

"I am."

"One time we went to Cali. But I wasn't singing yet."

"Ernesto was singing?"

"Yes. Ernesto was singing."

We didn't have any more time to talk because at that very instant Ricardo's father shouted from the door of the trailer.

"Ricardo!" he said, and we thought something had happened. And then: "Have you got a marker?" Ricardo nodded, said something about his jacket and the pocket of his jacket, and soon his father was approaching us. "What's your father's name?" I asked quietly. "Aurelio," he said. And Aurelio walked over as if he were in a hurry, carrying an accordion in his arms.

"It belongs to a fan," he said. "He wants us all to sign it."

He pulled over a chair, put the box on his lap like a baby, scribbled a dedication across the white of the keys, and said to no one: "Let's see if it plays." Right away, as he opened and closed the bellows, he explained (explained to no one, but obviously the explanation was meant for me) that he knew a few *vallenatos*, but his *vallenatero* accordion was at home, because it was too heavy to carry on long trips. "Sounds like it should," he then said of the signed accordion, and passed the marker to Ricardo.

"Where should I sign?" Ricardo asked.

"Wait, let's go in, so everyone can sign."

"Well, I'll sign it and then you can take it," Ricardo said.

Aurelio said no, that they should go to the dressing room, that it was time to warm up, they were all there, that didn't Ricardo like being with his family anymore, and then he let out a guffaw that echoed round the stone courtyard.

"Well, we'll see you in a bit," Ricardo said to me.

"Okay," I answered. "Let's see if we can talk for a while. I've talked to everyone except you."

"It's true," he said. "But don't take offense, man."

He walked away with a friendly smile, and I was left thinking that it was true, that I hadn't talked to him, that I'd talked to all of them except him. And then I thought: a singer never drinks cold water before a concert. And then I thought: it was not necessary to go to the dressing room to sign an accordion, especially if the accordion was here.

Don't take offense, man.

Ricardo went into one of the empty boxes on the second floor, sat down on the velvet seat, and looked at the ceiling: HONOR TO THE FINE ARTS was the legend floating among clouds and angels with trumpets, very close to the chandelier threatening to come loose and fall on top of the stalls. That afternoon, while all his uncles saw the sights of Málaga, Ricardo chose to stay in the hotel and then, nervous, as if Ernesto's blow still stung his cheek and kept him from resting, he went down to the lobby, asked some questions, and received a map, and walked, under the murderous midday sun, to the opera house where that night's concert would take place. He arrived sweating (his surname on a plastic card was enough for the theater's doorman to let him in the back door), and the sweat made his trousers stick to his skin, but the worst was the feeling of his skin sticking to the velvet. Ricardo endured it: he didn't stand up, he didn't go back downstairs, even though he was beginning to hear noises backstage, the metallic grinding of a door three meters high, the engine of the truck backing in to unload the lights and sound equipment, the sound engineer's instructions, that goes here, put that there. Today he wasn't prepared to give them a hand. Today he'd stay on the sidelines.

He stayed on the sidelines while the technicians set up the systems. He stayed on the sidelines while watching the band arrive one by one, stroll across the floorboards, and tune their instruments. He stayed on the sidelines during the rehearsal, which he listened to almost hidden in the theater box, without ever having the certainty that the Márquez Brothers were aware of his presence, because they never looked up and because the lights were shining in their faces. Ricardo didn't take his eyes off Ernesto Márquez, wearing narrow serge trousers and a short-sleeved shirt and the worn-out moccasins of an impoverished tourist. He realized he had started to despise him, and the more he looked at him the more he despised him, and a couple of times he closed his eyes just to search the singing voice for signs of deterioration and of pain. He realized he liked to remember the throat-clearing he had heard (that they'd all heard) the previous night, and he also liked to imagine the pain. After the final verses of the last corrido in Madrid, after singing *The friends from your land / do you wrong and do you harm / And you feel like a stranger / and the deception hurts,* Ricardo had noticed what all the rest of them noticed:

the reflex of a hand reaching for the throat, repenting halfway there, and going back under the accordion strap. Later, in the trailer, his father had gone over to Ernesto and placed an affectionate hand on his neck. And Ricardo had thought with no proof whatsoever: He's in pain. And he had felt happy that he was in pain.

And during the whole concert in the theater in Málaga, during the sad spectacle of mummies who go to hear corridos, sitting in velvet seats and paralyzed from the waist down, Ricardo heard the songs in the voice of his uncle Ernesto and amused himself by imagining the nature of the damage and wondering if he was really in pain, how much pain there was. Ernesto, like the best in his business, knew all the tricks available to take care of his voice, to avoid the most difficult notes in a way that was neither vulgar nor obvious, but that wasn't the important thing: the important thing, as Ricardo had said to his father on the bus between Madrid and Málaga, was that little by little Ernesto had renounced certain flourishes that a year ago (months ago) would have been characteristic. Little by little he was ceasing to be the vocalist of the Márquez Brothers; he was losing what distinguished him, and the group's identity was beginning to disappear with him. "Don't be insolent," his father had said. "He invented the group, he is our identity." "Do you really believe that?" Ricardo said, and his father didn't answer, which, for Ricardo, was undoubtedly the best answer. Ricardo was remembering that, he was reliving those words inside his distracted head, when he felt around him a curious emptiness he hadn't felt before, something like a displacement of air, and it took him a couple of seconds to realize that Ernesto Márquez had missed a note, or, rather, his throat had refused to give it to him.

Ernesto Márquez backed away from the microphone. Ricardo thought: he's going to cough. He's going to cough and the world is going to end.

But Ernesto took a deep breath, grimaced, and his eyes welled up. The band came to his rescue, singing the rest of the corrido in unison and saying good night at the end of it (doing what they'd never done: ending a concert early). The mummies, of course, didn't notice a thing, or it was to be expected that they hadn't noticed a thing, because barely a few minutes later they were clustered on the front steps of the theater, and when the Márquez Brothers came out they were met by a mob of hands reaching out with records and expecting autographs, and those without records had old photographs or tape recorders expecting a word or two for a provincial radio station. Afterward the whole band and their team were invited to the Juan y Mariano restaurant: a steep, narrow little street, a glass door, a badly lit and noisy place. Ernesto excused himself: he was tired, he said so everyone could hear him, he'd rather go back to the hotel early and have some honey and lemon and be refreshed for the rest of the journey. And the Márquezes watched him walk away alone to the next corner, suddenly an old man lost in the midst of the roving youthful party, a gray-ing head that stood out under the yellow lights of the Málaga streetlamps.

"This can't happen again," said Hugo.

"There's not much left," Ricardo's father said.

"It's just that this record—" Hugo said.

"Yes. But there's not much left. We have to finish the tour."

"And what if he doesn't finish it?"

"He's going to finish it," Ricardo's father said. "That's what we agreed."

"And if he can't? What if he doesn't finish it?"

Ricardo, in silence, was following close behind them.

In Cartagena, where we arrived at noon, the thermometer read forty-two degrees Celsius. The international music festi-val was taking place at the highest point in the city, a sort of amphitheater constructed on a mountaintop overlooking the Mediterranean; there, with winds blowing over the stone tiers, the temperature was two or three degrees lower than at sea level, and I can say I felt the change as I walked up—because I had decided to have lunch by myself and arrive under my own steam instead of taking advantage of the band's bus—as if as I climbed the rough asphalt I was taking off one layer of skin after another. I remember the temptation of not attend-ing the final concert, the resignation at having wasted a week traveling with people for whom I, visibly, was an annoyance and a nuisance at best, and an indiscreet person (almost a paparazzo, a literary paparazzo) at worst. But it was the last concert of the tour, just as it had been five years earlier: something ordered me to be there, to witness, as if my week with the Márquez Brothers were a house and I was the only one who had the keys to lock up after everyone had left. The entrance to the amphitheater was a brass door I found ajar. I went in and stayed awhile in front of the empty stage. The Márquez Brothers weren't there. I waited a bit longer. The Márquez Brothers were still absent.

I went up onstage by the side ladder and saw the traces of an interrupted rehearsal: they had been there, but they'd gone. Their instruments were on the black floorboards: the guitars, a saxophone, the abandoned accordion (the inner cushion soaked with Aurelio's sweat, a real aquatic stain that turned the red into the color of blood). At that moment Alonso entered the amphitheater, accompanied by one of the local organizers of the festival. One of the sound engineers, who had a rapper's name on his boots, came out to meet him; they were talking to each other, explaining things. I approached and asked them where everybody was and Alonso told me there had been a schedule change: they'd been asked to delay the concert, planned for nine, until eleven o'clock at night. "Eleven?" I said. Yes, eleven: because for the television people it was important that the end of the concert coincide with the fireworks, and the scheduled time of the fireworks, for reasons related to the live transmission in Latin America, had been changed this year and was immovable. "We're going to be here till late," Alonso said.

"And then?" I said.

"Then what?"

"Where is everyone?"

"At the hotel," Alonso said, "taking a break from the heat." And then: "Everyone except Ricardo, who's waiting for you."

He moved his head like an uncomfortable horse; I followed the movement and saw him: Ricardo was sitting in the last row of the amphitheater, in the shade of a colonnade that a couple of young men were beginning to adorn with Latin American flags. He's waiting for you, Alonso had said, and I had hidden my surprise and avoided asking why and since when. As I walked up the stairs I felt in my thighs and lungs the weight of the mountain I'd just climbed and also the violent heat. But when I reached Ricardo's side all that tiredness evaporated, and the shade of the colonnade was the sweetest I'd known in a long time. "We'll be more comfortable up here," Ricardo said. I sat down beside him, stretched out my legs the way he had his stretched out, and stayed there, like him, with my gaze fixed on the stage where the sound technicians were moving around and the instruments seemed to reverberate in the afternoon sun. And neither of us had to spark off the dialogue the way they do in bad plays, neither of us had to break the ice or execute those complicated steps with which two people approach a conversation they both desire, but neither knows how to get to. None of that happened. One moment we were in complete silence, two old friends who no longer need to fill their silences with banalities. The next moment, without any transition, Ricardo had begun to speak.

"It wasn't as hot as today," he said. "But it was hot. It was really hot. We were all uncomfortable, all sweating. We felt dirty, that's what it was, we felt dirty."

They had arrived the previous night, too late, from Málaga. On the bus, the Márquez brothers had behaved like belligerent spouses (in a marriage of four): they all pretended to be asleep so they wouldn't have to confront what had happened in the theater, what had happened to Ernesto's throat at the end of the concert. "Nobody's going to say anything to him?" Ricardo asked his father that night, in the dark hotel room. And his father too—lying a couple of yards away, in the other bed, his silhouette outlined by the light that filtered in under the door—had pretended to sleep. Ricardo imagined his uncle Ernesto standing in front of the bathroom mirror and holding a hand up to his neck or thinking of words such as *polyps*, or *nodes*, or *laryngeal cancer*. He fell asleep like that, and the next day he got up before his father and went down to the dining room at that time when in hotel dining rooms there are only bitter waiters and old insomniacs, that hour when all the newspapers are still on the table by the entrance, patient and virginal, because nobody has read them. And there, of course, was Ernesto Márquez, eating a croissant with little mouse bites. "There was nothing else on his plate," Ricardo told me. "And he was holding it with both hands, he had the croissant in both hands. A croissant is a very small thing, it's hard to hold it with two hands to put it in your mouth. But that's what my uncle was doing, and he was taking one of those mouse bites when I told him." Since the family wouldn't dare, Ricardo thought, it was up to him to tell him what they were all thinking.

"The family thinks it's about time you retired," Ricardo spat at his uncle. "The family wants you to go."

Ricardo had imagined a hundred different reactions. But he hadn't imagined the response his uncle Ernesto had in fact made. He didn't even raise his eyes from his plate covered in flecks of croissant.

"I already talked to the others," Ernesto said.

"You're finished, Uncle," Ricardo said. "It's as simple as that. We don't want you to keep on singing."

"I already talked to them," Ernesto repeated. And then: "I am going to sing this concert. It's going to be the last one. Then I'll leave you all in peace."

"Well, I disagree," Ricardo said. "This concert is a live recording. This concert is going to be broadcast all over Latin America."

"You little prick," Ernesto said with a kind of urgency—no,

violence—Ricardo had never seen. "Nobody cares what you think." And then: "I am going to sing this concert, that's all. And if you don't like it, you can go to hell."

Ricardo spent the day away from the band and also from the crew, hiding and fleeing without admitting to himself that he was hiding and fleeing, and in the background weighing up the reactions of the family. Reproaches would come, his father's disavowal, accusations; they would call him insolent (he was used to that), they would talk of hierarchies and lines and who had the right to cross them. Ricardo walked aimlessly through the scorching city, taking refuge from the heat in supermarkets—pausing at length in front of the freezers—spending the last minutes before the concert down by the port, watching the boats, distracting his mind. The sky turned purple and then gray and then the outlines of things disappeared and then the light from the streetlamps turned everything yellow, and when he raised his head Ricardo saw that up there, on the mountain, was a distant brilliance. He concentrated, tried to hear the music, to detect the vibrations of the bass; he believed, without too much conviction, that he could. Facing the black hole of the sea, he sang the songs. "The Beast." "The Powerful Ones." "Shadows in My Soul." He sang the next one, "The Virgin of the Poor," from the first verse to the last. And then he sang three more, calculating not only their exact timings, which wasn't difficult for him, but also the time between them, the routines of silence and pauses contained in that concert he'd heard since birth and which by that moment were imprinted in his consciousness as clearly as his own name. And then, as slowly as he could, he began walking up.

He was not surprised that his calculations (that is: his ear) gave him perfect results. Ricardo was walking along the wall of the amphitheater at the same time as the final beats of the last corrido—*And you feel like a stranger*, the audience sang along, *and the deception hurts*—and he showed his plastic card to the security guard at the same time as the Márquez Brothers left the stage. He mixed with the members of the audience standing between the edge of the stage and the first row of seats, making his way with difficulty toward the center of the crowd and feeling the elbows and hips that bumped against him. Then the Márquezes came back onstage, this time without any instruments. They raised their hands, waved to the audience, and the sky lit up. Fireworks? thought Ricardo. He didn't know they were planned. But why should he have known if he was absent all afternoon, if that afternoon he was no longer a Márquez. Yes, he thought that: I am no longer one of them. He didn't think it would hurt so much.

When they arrived at the hotel, the fireworks were still lighting up the night. Flashes of color were exploding in the very black sky, and Ricardo thought of the crafts he did as a child, at school, when the teacher asked him to color a piece of paper using crayons and then cover the whole thing with a layer of black, so afterward, if he scratched the surface with a pin, the colors emerged from the background like the red, blue, and green lights now emerging from the background of the sky. That was what he was thinking when his father took him by the arm and led him to the hotel bar, where a man was cleaning glasses and getting ready to close. Ricardo noticed that Alonso and Hugo had also followed them: the only one who'd gone to rest, without even saying good night to Ricardo, was Uncle Ernesto. They asked for a bottle of tequila and four glasses, and only when his father was filling his with a strange solemnity, only when there was silence at that table where there was never silence, did Ricardo know that this wasn't an end-of-tour toast, but something very different. Then he heard his father speak.

His father told him what had happened after the Málaga concert without Ricardo's knowledge. They had returned from the Juan y Mariano restaurant and gone to bed; at three in the morning, the telephone rang in Hugo's room. It was Ernesto, who was calling them one by one to summon them to a meeting in his room: all of them, except Ricardo. So, in pajamas and on the unmade bed of the eldest brother, between those walls that smelled of insomnia, they listened to Ernesto talk. And Ernesto apologized to them, stone-faced, his voice slow and deliberate, somewhat resigned, but also guilty: for not having told them earlier, for having hidden information that concerned the whole family. Three months after the diagnosis of laryngeal cancer, the doctors had given him the news he didn't want to hear: they were going to remove his cancerous larynx. Ernesto asked what would happen if he refused, what would happen if he kept his diseased larynx, and they told him: "You'll die before Christmas." They were telling him he'd have a longer life, but Ernesto begged like a man condemned to death: he begged them to delay the surgery until after the tour of Spain, to be able to sing the last concerts, to be able to leave his inheritance to his family, but also to his fans. And the doctors agreed. The surgery was scheduled for the following Friday.

"Next Friday," Ricardo's father said, "Ernesto will no longer have a voice. He's not going to sing, he's not going to speak. Never again, Ricardo. A fucking mime, that's what he's going to be."

"He's not going to talk?" Ricardo said.

"They're going to take all this out," his father said, holding his hand to his throat in the shape of a claw and tugging on his Adam's apple. "He's going to spend the rest of his life in silence, I don't know if you realize."

"I didn't know," Ricardo said.

"Nobody knew," his father said. "Ernesto didn't want to tell us. After Málaga, he had to."

"He thought we weren't going to let him sing the last concert," Hugo said. "And the truth is we were considering it."

Ricardo hadn't touched his tequila. "It was the last concert," he said, "and I wasn't there."

"Imagine, *güey*," Hugo said. "All these days he was giving himself shots of cortisone, all alone, in his room. Injecting them on his own, he's a tough bastard."

"I'll never hear him sing again," Ricardo said.

"Well, no," his father said. "But you brought that on yourself. You brought it on and you missed it."

He told me all that there, in the last tier of the amphitheater, shortly before the last concert on the 2001 tour. The heat had let up slightly, but it was still possible to feel on your head and shoulders the weight of the whole day's sun. "You understand, don't you?" he said. I said yes, I did understand, but the truth is I didn't know what he was referring to. I couldn't understand that burden, couldn't understand the way the figure of Ernesto Márquez had accompanied his heir these last five years, nor could I understand what they must feel—all of them, not just his heir—repeating those steps now, the songs, the routines of that sad year 1996.

"And what happened to Ernesto?" I asked.

When they returned from the Spanish tour, when they landed in Los Angeles, three days before Ernesto lost his voice forever, they had a long and complicated meeting with the doctors, resembling a negotiation more than anything else. They tried to keep the doctors from performing a tracheotomy on Ernesto. It was the most conventional surgery, but

Ernesto preferred not to go around with a hole in his throat for the rest of his life. The tracheotomy, Ricardo explained, would have allowed him to speak through an electrical apparatus, a sort of plug they put in the hole, but would prevent him from playing his harmonica ever again. "I'm not going to play it with my throat," Ernesto told the doctors. The doctors agreed; over the next few days, the whole family made a list of useful or usual expressions: the things Ernesto would need to say most often, but that he couldn't say with signals. Then they went to the studio where they'd recorded all their albums and Ernesto pronounced the phrases into a microphone, and these phrases were put into a special tape recorder they gave to the doctors. At the press of a button Ernesto's voice would say *We have to settle up* or *A rooster's always crowing* or *Sooner or later* or *My tequila's evaporated* or *Don't pay any attention if I get angry.* Then came the surgery and Ernesto's voice ceased to exist in the world, except for the set phrases that came out of the tape recorder.

"Ernesto died a couple of years ago," he then told me. "At the end of 1999. He didn't get to see the new century, but he did get to hold the live album of the tour in his hands."

The album. His brothers (and his nephew) took him a copy one evening, hot off the press. Ernesto greeted them with a smile and a phrase sounded from his tape recorder: *Evening, boys. What brings you here?* But he turned serious when he saw what they'd brought him. They sat in the studio that Ernesto had had built years before, when he had money for the first time, and the Márquez Brothers' corridos filled the air.

"And we listened to the Cartagena concert from the first song to the last," Ricardo told me. "Together there, the whole family. I could only think that I'd sung those songs in my head that evening, walking up the mountain to the theater, toward this theater. I'd sung all those songs in my head, but without hearing them, or rather, hearing them in the distance. And meanwhile, Ernesto had sung them knowing he'd never sing them again."

Ricardo stood up. He said he was going to go change and put on the headphones and warm up a bit before the others arrived. And then he left me alone.

And this is what has stayed with me of that tour with the Márquez Brothers and that other tour I didn't witness, but which Ricardo told me about in detail and which I've been able to reconstruct. The image of Ernesto Márquez, whom I never met, has stayed with me, sitting in the music room of his house in Los Angeles surrounded by his family, hearing his own voice on the album of the tour, and hearing it as only he could hear it, because nobody hears our own voice the way we hear it ourselves, because our voices sound different inside our heads when we speak, so we're always surprised when we hear it outside of us: in a message on the answering machine, on a video someone has taken of us, in a song we've sung knowing it was the last. And what Ricardo said when he was already on his feet, before saying goodbye, has stayed with me. That evening when the family was listening to the brand-new record of the Cartagena concert, when they reached the end of the last corrido and Ernesto Márquez, accompanied by his brothers, was singing the lines from the speakers, something happened that no one had foreseen. Ernesto picked up his machine of set phrases; his fingers moved over the buttons, and his eyes fixed on Ricardo while his recorded voice said:

Now you sing it.

SONGS FOR THE FLAMES

This is the saddest story I have ever heard, as a novelist once said of his, and in this one it all starts with a book, contrary to what a poet said. Actually, it's not one story, but several; or a story with several beginnings, at least, although it has only one ending. And I must control them all, all the beginnings or all the stories, so none may escape, because the truth could be in any of them, the timid truth I'm looking for in the middle of these outrageous events.

A few years ago, in the middle of 2014, I found myself lost in the writing of a stubborn, complex novel about many things, but in particular about two: the murders, more shadowy than our obstinate history would like to admit, of Rafael Uribe Uribe and Jorge Eliécer Gaitán. I was spending long hours in the Luis Ángel Arango Library, a labyrinthine building in my city, documenting the known truth about those crimes but, especially, looking for documents that told or hinted at a different truth, hidden or forgotten, a buried or secret truth. I was also spending hard hours, generally late and nocturnal, getting lost in other labyrinths: the labyrinths of the internet, which have never stopped causing me a profound anxiety whose symptoms, as far as I've been able to discover, are very similar to those of agoraphobia. A long time later, when this story was already finished and I was beginning to try to understand it, someone explained to me the role algorithms had played in all of this. By mechanisms I haven't bothered to retain, my search history caused me to receive a commercial offer one day. From Santiago de Chile, a dealer in rare and antique books offered me a signed first edition of a volume the existence of which I knew nothing about: a grammar book by Rafael Uribe Uribe.

The book arrived by post thirty days later. Uribe Uribe had written or compiled it when he was just over twenty-five years old, while spending several months in prison for murder. Another civil war had broken out; Uribe Uribe had put himself at the head of the Liberal forces of Antioquia; after a threat of insurrection in his troops, the colonel—because Uribe Uribe was a colonel by then—took the soldier responsible for the insubordination and shot him personally and without any form of trial. His Conservative enemies, victorious in the war, did not squander the chance to imprison him for a year, while a judge decided his fate. In the end he was absolved, but he used that year in prison to write this volume I now had in my hands: an *Abridged Dictionary of Gallicisms, Provincialisms, and Language Corrections* that the author or compiler dedicated, so there would be no doubt about the earnestness of his intentions, to the most prestigious grammarian of the day: Rufino José Cuervo.

The dictionary was published in a country that was already conservative, not by temperament, which it always has been, but by law: the new constitution, which would govern the country for a whole century plus five years, had been enacted the previous year "in the name of God, supreme source of all authority"; it declared Catholicism the only official religion, protected "by the public powers" and "respected as the essential element of social order" and tolerated other denominations as long as they weren't "contrary to Christian morality." Uribe Uribe, in response to the new order, founded the liberal newspaper *La Disciplina*; but later he was imprisoned again, in large part for having founded the liberal newspaper *La Disciplina*. In light of all that, it is not unusual that he should have devoted the following years to civilian life: he founded his own coffee plantation in Antioquia, Gualanday, and administered other people's coffee plantations in Cundinamarca and in old Caldas and the future Quindío; he read, he wrote, he worried about the fate of the country; he met new people, got on well with some of them, was hated by others.

He wanted, in short, to be just another citizen, a farmer of uncertain fortune and head of a family of firm convictions and quick indignations, yes, but far from public life.

He did not manage it, as is well-known. Another war came along at the end of the century, the cruelest and bloodiest of all; after the war, having learned its lessons and that of the suffering he'd witnessed in it, Uribe turned into a man of peace; and thus he earned the hatred of his friends, who called him a traitor and sellout, while he kept his old enemies, who called him an atheist and a socialist. On October 15, 1914, shortly after midday, two tradesmen smashed his skull with hatchets on the busiest street in Bogotá.

Of that whole life, what interests me now—what is pertinent to my sad story—is the time he spent as an amateur farmer. For one of the haciendas he administered, although for a very short time, was that of the De León family: ten privileged hectares in the Cocora Valley from the boundaries of which you could see, running through a mountain cleft that left walkers breathless, a stream so wide it could have been called a river. The hacienda was called Nueva Lorena: an incongruous and even pompous name, but one that corresponded to the family's temperament as only our defects can. Uribe Uribe took charge of it for four or five months of the year 1898. The new civil war, which could already be seen coming over the horizon, interrupted his labors. Or that's what we can suppose, at least; otherwise, it's impossible to understand why he would have given up that perfect job where the coffee grew itself and there was time to read and write with no interference: since the owners, the De Leóns and their young son, were abroad, and nothing seemed to indicate they would soon return to Colombia.

Whatever the case, Uribe Uribe resigned from the De Leóns' farm, but not from the epistolary friendship that had sprung up between them. In his letters, he asked Jorge de León to write to him of the latest literary news; Jorge de León tells him that he is a businessman and knows little of the arts, but his wife and son were both aficionados; in one letter there is a mention of Maurice Barrès; in another, now well into the new century, the García Calderón brothers, who published a magazine about Latin America. I envy the richness of your lives, writes Uribe Uribe in a moment of grandiloquence. Here, instead, it is an immense desert.

The De León family, Jorge and Beatriz, had settled in Paris at the end of the 1870s. There in the 16th Arrondissement, a few blocks from the business that allowed them a life of luxury, their son, Gustavo Adolfo, was born. At the age of twenty-one, when this young man who had never set foot in Colombia had to choose between his two possible nationalities, he chose to be Colombian, perhaps seduced by the fascination of a remote place, perhaps tricked by his loyalty to his parents; but he did not neglect to note that in the case of France going to war, he would enlist to fight with the Foreign Legion. Had he imagined how close the conflagration was? Maybe he hadn't, but his parents had. In June of 1914, when Gavrilo Princip assassinated Archduke Franz Ferdinand and his wife on a Sarajevo street, the De Leóns began to consider an idea: something very big and very serious was going to happen here, and maybe it was time to consider the possibility of returning to Colombia. A month later, a member of Action Française, irritated by the combat Jean Jaurès was leading against the monstrosities of war, irritated by the warnings Jaurès was delivering on the risks of military alliances, excited by the conservative propaganda that was calling Jaurès a dog and a traitor and unpatriotic and a socialist and an atheist, found him while he was having lunch and shot him dead from the sidewalk. The crime, which shook Paris, surprised the De Leóns with one foot on the boat, and helped them recognize it was time to leave Europe.

But their son refused to follow them. In August he already knew his destiny: the Second Marching Regiment of the First Foreign Legion. By the time his parents were arriving at the coffee plantation, after crossing the Atlantic from Le Havre and making uncomfortable ports of call and arriving in Barranquilla and sailing up the Magdalena on a steamship and driving up the mountains from the river port in a sprung carriage, Gustavo Adolfo was already making himself as comfortable as possible in an inhospitable train fifty coaches long and traveling to Bayonne to complete his training. In his letters, the boredom of the beginning turned into the excitement of his first simulated maneuvers and the first simulated attacks. His parents received this information with anxiety, but the war, for news of which they had to go to the city, always seemed too far away, or the demands of the hacienda filled their days and prevented them from keeping up. By letter, they announced their arrival to Uribe Uribe, and he answered them from Bogotá in a jubilant tone and promised a visit as soon as his obligations in the Senate of the Republic allowed. He never managed to fulfill that promise: the tradesmen and their hatchets prevented it.

Yesterday they killed General Uribe as well, Jorge de León wrote to his son. The world is going crazy. The letter reached him just a couple of days before he left Bayonne for the Mailly-Champagne encampment, where his company joined up with the Moroccan Division under the orders of Colonel Pein. Gustavo Adolfo painstakingly gave his parents all these particulars; he also told them of the hard work he'd never been used to, of his pride in defending civilization from barbarity, of the refuges made of earth with straw roofs where platoons of rats made their homes. Toward the end of the year, his letters filled with references to trenches, the thundering of shells, and the bullets that whistled past, Gustavo Adolfo said, like cats in heat. He spoke with pride of having dug an exemplary trench able to withstand an attack by the Boches, and of a Venezuelan friend who had been hit in the head by shrapnel and whose luck seemed to have run out. If he survives, Gustavo Adolfo wrote, he'll be worse off. In that letter he complains of the legionnaires' abuse of the French language, that beautiful language that is his language, the language of Molière and Flaubert. And it is impossible to know this and not think of another letter, written in Champagne on April 22, in which he announces that he'll be leaving for a new position in a matter of days and thanks his parents effusively for the gift they have sent him. It was Rafael Uribe Uribe's *Diccionario*, beside the title of which his mother has written (the calligraphy is decidedly feminine) a few solemn lines: *To our hero with the desire to see you soon and celebrate together the victory on the fields of honor.*

A few days later he was digging trenches in Artois. He realized that others had already been working on them for several days, and that a great battle was looming. Of what happened to him later there is no news, but we know how the confrontation played out. On May 9, at dawn, an artillery bombardment commenced the attack. His company's mission was to take what they called the White Works, a ridge of uneven terrain where the Germans had carved into the chalky hillsides, near the Berthonval Wood, and then to take Hill 140. The regiment's performance was miraculous: supported by snipers, the infantrymen launched themselves against the camp with suicidal enthusiasm, as if that were the last battle, and in a matter of an hour and a half they had achieved their objective. They did not lose too many men, but one of the ones they did lose, killed instantly by a bullet through his neck, was Gustavo Adolfo de León, who would have turned twenty-six on Sunday of the following week.

Among the dead soldier's papers, which were swiftly sent to his family, they found some lines of verse that might have come from an unfinished sonnet.

Each inferno suggests a private genesis:
Its own purgat'ry, its intrinsic reprimand.
Inferno is the trench where the enemy burns;
Purgatory, the flesh of the quiet woman.

The debt to Rubén Darío (those proparoxytones, those alexandrines) is more than evident, or that's what I thought from the start. De León had published the odd poem in the London magazine edited by the diplomat and writer Santiago Pérez Triana; Pérez Triana, who corresponded with Joseph Conrad and Miguel de Unamuno, was a friend or at least a colleague of Rubén Darío, and it is not impossible that he might have recommended readings to the soldier poet. The quatrain is not unassailable, but it is suggestive: the young idealist, the good son, the sacrificing patriot, was also capable of a worldly life. Other lines, written in the margin of a ministerial letter with neither punctuation nor rhyme, speak of the same thing:

> *Your breasts are the field of my sacrifice*
> *The shape of your lips my homeland of choice*

I put myself in the place of his parents, who at the end of 1915 open this parcel of their dead son's letters and papers, and I try to imagine them in the act of receiving the news, of absorbing the blow. And I fail: I don't know how Gustavo Adolfo's parents received the blow (absorbed the news) there, on the coffee plantation. In that parcel were the letters they had sent him, but they would have missed the *Dictionary of Gallicisms*. I know it was not in the parcel because it arrived later, six years later, and not by a route they would have expected.

I imagine it like a scene from Faulkner: the beginning of *Light in August*, for example, although here it's not a pregnant young woman looking for the father of her baby, but an older man who brings a little girl by the hand. They walked from Salento: he is wearing a tropical suit; he has the girl by one hand and a heavy suitcase in the other; and I like to think he would have loosened his tie and draped his jacket over the little girl's shoulders, because I know they arrived at dusk and it's possible the girl would have been cold. It was October 1921, Jorge and Beatriz were sitting at the table, waiting for their frugal supper to be served, when the dogs began to bark. The iron bell that hung on the front door rang; Jorge gave an order and someone went downstairs to ask who it was and what they wanted at that hour. Minutes later, without even having brushed the dust off their shoes, the stranger and the little girl were sitting at the table with the De Leóns, in front of plates of rice and beans, the man trying to explain between mouthfuls that he'd had a hell of a time finding the Nueva Lorena Hacienda, that his destination was Bogotá and he was doing this charitable task that he couldn't understand himself. The girl had recently turned six, had very white skin and blue eyes she seemed to hide out of shyness. Allow me to introduce your granddaughter, the man said, and then he told them what had happened so that the two of them ended up arriving here.

The man's name was Silva, he was a homeopathic doctor and he was coming from Nicaragua and Panama. He had arrived at Cartagena after traveling for several months; he took the train to Calamar and there boarded the same steamship—the *Díez Hernando*—on which the little girl and her mother were sailing. He was immediately on good terms with the woman. Madame Dumontet, as the woman introduced herself, was talkative and open, and talking to her was not only easy, but agreeable; of course, for her it was also a pleasure, not to mention a stroke of luck, to meet someone who spoke French, even if it was a mediocre French with an island accent. In a few hours the man had learned that Madame Dumontet lived in Paris, and this was not only the first time she'd crossed the Atlantic, but the first time she'd been outside the borders of France. She was going to Colombia to meet the family of her husband, she explained more than once, a war hero who had died for France in the battle of Artois; but traveling alone was not easy, and although the trip had gone without problems as far as reaching the Caribbean, now she was beginning to feel tired. She'd spent three days on terra firma waiting for this steamship to leave! A torrential rain fell on us, she said, I have never seen it rain like that. The first night we were devoured by mosquitoes, if you look at this poor little girl's leg, it's all swollen. You do not know, monsieur, what my daughter and I felt when we heard the ship's siren. Silva looked at her. Madame Dumontet could not be more than thirty years old: widow of a war hero, mother of a fatherless child, and here she was, venturing through unknown lands to give her daughter a family: was it not admirable? Well, now we're on board, Silva said to her, now it's just a matter of relaxing and enjoying the scenery: wait till you see this landscape. And she said yes, she was admiring it.

The boat left at five in the afternoon, and by half past six everyone was in their cabins. The next morning, after a night plagued by mosquitoes and during which the heat would not let him sleep, Silva arrived at breakfast to discover that the Frenchwoman was ill. A group of benevolent passengers accompanied the little girl while she drank a milky coffee and ate a couple of slices of bread, but the coffee was disgusting and the butter was rancid and smelled like fish, so Silva ran to his room and came back with a tin of biscuits. What's your name? he asked the little girl. She didn't answer. Do you like the boat? he asked. It's like a turtle, the girl said, and then added: Mamá is sick. Her head hurts. She'll get better, Silva told her, the tropics are always difficult for someone visiting for the first time. Do you want to go and see the chickens? The girl's face lit up. Are there chickens? she exclaimed. Silva took her by the hand and they went down the stairs and walked between the trunks and beside the boilers and arrived at some cages to see the chickens. There were five or six, and Silva was sure they wouldn't be enough for the week's travel they had ahead of them, but he didn't even tell the little girl that these nice chickens would be in her soup one of these days.

That night, after dinner, when he was comfortable in his cabin and getting ready for bed, Silva heard someone knocking on his door. It was the captain, who came to ask him personally if he would look after the Frenchwoman. She's burning up, the captain said. Silva got dressed again and went to the cabin where Madame Dumontet was moaning and writhing, and the first thing he noticed was the strong odor of vomit.

He had trouble accepting that the chattering he could hear was the springs and screws of the camp bed, which moved at the same time as the woman's convulsed body, or rather were moved by the shivering of her ailing body. Silva placed his hand on her cheek and his hand was drenched in fresh sweat. He did not remember, in all his travels, ever having felt such a high fever. He untied the knot at the neck of her nightdress. On the shelf he found two embroidered towels; he soaked them both in the water of the washbasin and used one to cover her neck and chest, and with the other he made a sort of glove to wipe her inflamed forehead and fiery cheeks. Then he brought a dose of quinine to her cabin, because he didn't know what else to do, and he told Madame Dumontet that she'd feel better the next day.

And she did feel better; in fact, she even asked for something to eat, but then she said she had a terrible thirst and began to drink so much water that he had to fill the porcelain jug in her cabin five times over the course of the day. Silva went down to the filter and waited patiently while the stone cleaned the murky river water, and then he went back up to give the jug to the patient. He came to believe, after one of those visits, that Madame Dumontet would recover, because he saw her conversing animatedly with another woman. He went to sleep thinking about that: it had just been indigestion, yes, something in the water, the bacteria, the microbes that swarmed in these places so far from the hand of Pasteur. Deep down he knew there were other more frightful possibilities, because he had seen similar symptoms in Colón and in the Gulf. And his worst presentiments were confirmed at dawn, when he emerged from his cabin and found a small army of aprons trying to clean Madame Dumontet's dark vomit from the wooden floor.

Twenty-four hours later—after much vomiting, after high fevers and much sweat and many futile remedies—she was dead. They wrapped her in her own sheets, Silva told them, and a priest came and blessed her and prayed next to the ladder at the stern, and then they all put her on a board and let the body fall into the Magdalena and disappear from view while they advanced up river at the speed of someone walking along the bank. The little girl witnessed none of this, since someone had the good sense to distract her in a cabin, but later they explained to her that her mother had died and that now this gentleman would take her to see her family, and consoled her with words that had no visible effect. The worst, Silva said, was the quarantine: because then the boat had to dock at the first available port and raise the flag, and stay there for days that felt like years, during which coexistence deteriorated and the passengers grew impatient, and Silva had even broken the nose of a man who had insulted the girl whose mother was to blame for everything. Traveling alone with a daughter, the man had said: must've been a whore. But he said it in Spanish, and the girl didn't understand any of it.

And here we are, Silva said. Almost two months after having disembarked in Calamar. I don't know why this fell to me, but nor do I see how I could have refused. The little girl was alone, alone in an unknown country, unable to communicate with anyone and not knowing where to go. Luckily her mother was talkative, luckily she wasn't one of those timid passengers who doesn't talk to anyone, because at least I found out where to bring her. The Nueva Lorena Hacienda: many people had heard of the Nueva Lorena Hacienda, but these people, believe me, were not on board the *Díez Hernando* steamship. Anyway, here is your granddaughter: the child of your son, hero of the battle of Artois. Here is your granddaughter and here is your granddaughter's suitcase, as heavy as a deadweight, forgive me. I, for my part, request a night's lodging, and tomorrow I'll continue on my way to Bogotá.

And then he opened the suitcase right there, on the dining room table, and took out what he thought most important. It was a bundle of different-sized and -colored envelopes tied together with a ribbon: the letters that Gustavo Adolfo had written to the woman. But his parents, peering into the suitcase, found something else. Nestled among clothing and shoes was the *Dictionary of Gallicisms*. His mother opened the book and saw the inscription she had written in her own hand. And what is the little girl's name? she asked then.

Aurélie, Silva said. You can give her whatever surname you want.

Aurelia would be better, said Doña Beatriz. So she can be Colombian without having to explain anything.

And Aurelia de León spent the next four years at the Nueva Lorena, with her grandparents, getting lost among the coffee bushes, running down and climbing up the steep hillsides to help the pickers, slowly learning to speak the workers' Spanish. She also learned to squeeze the fruit to get the bean out and eat the sweet pulp until her stomach hurt, and she learned how to hang on the wheel of the smaller coffee mill to put it in motion. Her grandparents never knew how Gustavo Adolfo and the child's mother had met, because that information was not in the letters, but they did yield to the evidence that the relationship had not been a one-off thing: the soldier who stops over in Paris between two expeditions looking for women to alleviate the solitude or the fear. Among the letters there was one photo: the woman would probably have sent it to Gustavo Adolfo, but in the years of Nueva Lorena it enabled the grandparents to keep an image of her mother in the little girl's memory (even though it was a poor image, more of a blur than anything else).

That's how Aurelia de León grew up. When she turned ten, her grandparents decided they could not keep her living like a savage, surrounded by goats and plantains, at the mercy of the coffee pickers' worst instincts. They sent her to a Catholic boarding school in Bogotá, so the nuns of La Presentación would turn her into a good citizen.

———————

The second beginning to this story that has several, or the thread of which comes from different skeins, happened two years after the first. In the middle of 2016, my friend Jay, photographer of the Colombian war and inveterate traveler, called me to propose an article. She had the photos; she just needed the text. Jay then revealed to me the existence of a place I'd never heard of: the Free Cemetery of Circasia. While I listened to the explanations and tales Jay was pitching me over the phone, one after the other, as if leaving a second of silence was going to give me the chance to say no, and while I was mentally going over my commitments and obligations in the coming weeks, I thought that this country of mine will never stop surprising me. I immediately accepted and two weeks later made the trip.

The Free Cemetery was on a curve of a mountain road, on a little hill that seemed to rise up out of the edge of a driveway designed for visitors to leave their cars. It was the invention or creation of a group of impious folk back in the 1930s, mostly Freemasons, who set themselves the task of constructing a place where the remains of all those the Church refused could repose: atheists, communists, whores, suicides. One of them, the intellectual author of this place of rebellion, was called Braulio Botero, and there was his bust, welcoming me beneath the trees. It was drizzling when I arrived, and a cold wind blew every once in a while, bringing the temperature down five degrees with every gust, but none of that bothered me or even made me uncomfortable: my fascination was unshaken by the elements. I knew by then who Don Braulio was; I knew that his uncle Valerio Londoño, who had spent his whole life raising his voice against the priests and denouncing the Church's monopoly over children's education, had died around 1928; I knew that the local parish priest, Manuel Antonio Pinzón, had refused to allow him to be buried in the Cemetery of the Angels, and that Don Braulio had to travel around the area looking for a place that would accept his atheist free-thinking uncle. He didn't know until it was too late: Pinzón had telegraphed all the parishes in the area, from Filandia to Calarcá, so that none of them would commit the sacrilege of allowing him in. The family ended up returning to Circasia with the dead man's bones and burying them, with no ceremony apart from the ceremony of defeat, in the garden of their house.

Braulio Botero took up the gauntlet. He acquired a suitable piece of land, a gift from his father, and organized dances and bazaars to raise the five hundred pesos the work would cost. The most liberal ladies donated their jewels as their mothers had donated theirs for the last civil war, although they made very sure their names did not appear publicly among the donors, and a German engineer supervised the work without charging a single peso. They constructed four vertical vaults, so the founders of the cemetery would spend eternity on their feet, and adorned them with the same Masonic symbols I've seen elsewhere. (I did not find, however, any crosses, or statues of saints, or biblical verses anywhere.) Later I learned the rank of the founding Botero: Grand Knight Kadosh of the White and Black Eagle. I also learned that Jorge Eliécer Gaitán had visited the cemetery in the early 1930s, when the presidency of the country had returned to Liberal hands for the first time in forty-four years. I knew that the first person buried there was a German Lutheran who had been stabbed to death by a local Catholic in a dark alley. I did not know, however, who the most recent was.

Before leaving, having filled several pages of my notebook and having talked for almost half an hour with a man who was sweeping the paths and getting ready to wash the statues and plaques, I walked to one of the cemetery walls. The sound of children had caught my attention, children playing, sounding too close not to pique my curiosity, but too far away to be within the cemetery. I then discovered that, on the other side of the white wall, a few yards from these secular or agnostic or out-cast dead, there was a playground. A real one: with swings and slides and seesaws that left the smell of rust on your skin. All sorts of stupid metaphors went through my head about this proximity, but I had the good sense not to write any of them down in my notebook. And when I was about to leave, when I was already starting to walk away from the wall, I went past a monkey puzzle tree the base of which was painted white, according to a custom I've never seen in any other country in the world, and I noticed it had a bronze plaque on the trunk.

NEAR THIS LOCATION

AURELIA DE LEÓN

(1915–1949)

HAD HER FINAL RESTING PLACE

"IF YOU BRING LOTS OF MUSIC,

THAT RINGS OUT IN HADES . . ."

Beneath the inscription, in the bottom right corner of the plaque, I could just make out a burnished date: 1973.

Everything on the plaque was mysterious: Why had Aurelia de León had her final resting place near there, and why did she not have it anymore? Why had she died so young? Why had this plaque been put up so many years later, and who had put it here? What was the significance of the line of verse? I recognized it immediately: it was from "Warning to the Impertinent," one of those poems that are like secular prayers for me. I looked up the line on my phone to get a better idea of the context (these machines have obliterated patience and the effort of memory from our habits, for all the answers are there all the time) and found the whole poem on several sites, and found the mutilated or gutted poem on others: that's the risk poems run when they become popular. And then I came across, a few pages farther down, a quote that didn't mention the poet León de Greiff, but rather the existence of a book written in Spanish that used the line as an epigraph. The title was *Songs for the Flames*; the date of publication, 1975; the author, a certain Gustavo Adolfo de León.

And then I began to investigate.

I could not—have not been able to—find out how Aurelia de León's boarding school years went, but I imagine (nothing prevents me from imagining, given what happened later) a turbulent adolescence, an emergence into the world similar to the moment a kidnapping victim recovers her liberty. I have discovered, however, that her grandfather died a natural death while she was away at boarding school, and that Aurelia did not wish to return to Nueva Lorena even to attend the funeral at the Cemetery of the Angels. When she finished secondary school, she chose to stay in Bogotá, a city she'd barely glimpsed through windows, living an orphan's life with the family of Soledad Echavarría: two veterans of the war against the nuns (as they called themselves) who understood and protected and accompanied each other, and the welcoming family could not have been prouder to have a European young lady under their roof. Aurelia soon learned to use her origins, her mother tongue, and her blue eyes to project a lineage she lacked; in that, but not only in that, she had understood, as an outstanding student, the workings of a society that was now hers.

The Echavarrías lived in a neighborhood of English-style houses with steep, pointed, red-tile roofs, as if it might be necessary for snow to slide off in this city. There, in the attic, they took in Aurelia de León, and they did so convinced they were fulfilling a pedagogical or civilizing mission: it would be a waste if a young lady of such lively intelligence had to marry some small-town man. Señor Echavarría was an engineer who wore three-piece suits and gloves and carried an umbrella, born in the city and incapable of understanding there might be life outside it, or that people might enjoy descending from the high plateau to inhospitable places where they coexisted with strangers who had dark armpits and too much skin uncovered. He bombarded Aurelia de León with sermons or political speeches about the virtues of the city. Here, in the capital, was a suitable husband for her: someone able to talk about wines and the history of Byzantium, but also able to find the Manhattan shop where the best hats are sold. And if his wife, from the kitchen, said he didn't need to exaggerate, that sometimes it was nice to see a bit of green, he replied: Green, my love? As if we were forest rangers.

Aurelia de León took a few months to turn into part of the family. At first she was Soledad's chaperone, but that stopped when it was noticed that the suitors paid less attention to

Soledad than to her. Aurelia wore her beauty in a distracted way, like a shawl we grab in a hurry on the way out of the house, but she began to realize other things. At social gatherings, Sunday *ajiaco* suppers or literary *tertulias* the lady of the house organized at teatime, Aurelia would suddenly find herself at the center of the circle. She discovered that this did not make her uncomfortable. She spoke of her father's death as if she had been in the trenches of Artois, filling her tale with well-chosen details and dialogue in appropriate places, and she could tell the story of her mother's trip to the Americas and also of her illness and death in such a way that her audience—all those ladies whose cups of tea never lost their balance on their saucers—invariably ended up sobbing. Aurelia de León discovered a pleasure she'd never felt before: that of all those eyes on her, that of the silence that made way for her tale, that of the sudden gasps and the ladies bolt upright in their chairs with hands clutched together in their laps. The attention from the women made her feel a new sort of density, as if her body had affirmed itself on the earth. Sometimes, at gatherings where there were also men present, Señor Echavarría would ask her to tell her life story—that's how he said it: come on, dear, tell them the story of your life—and Aurelia de León took note that the looks in the eyes of the men were different, and that they liked her, and that the women's looks changed as well: they turned hostile, cunning, scrutinizing.

They were years of discovery: day after day, Aurelia de León found herself, or invented a version of herself, increasingly to her liking. The newspapers talked about her: they found her in society salons, listening to a poet's lecture, or took her photo in a house in San Victorino, and Aurelia de León would appear on the page surrounded by a committee in support of Jorge Eliécer Gaitán and above the caption "Liberal Ladies." Soledad's father thought such company questionable, to put it mildly: was she becoming a bad influence, this foreigner in sheep's clothing? In its "Women's Section," *Cromos* magazine revealed during those days something that Aurelia had kept scrupulously secret:

> New Faces.—Is journalism in Bogotá still in the hands of men? At least one audacious woman seems to be determined to prove otherwise. Readers of *El Espectador* might not know it but the social page their eyes run over every day is presided over by Señorita Aurelia de León, French by birth, who for some time now has been gracing our salons with her beauty. Señorita De León registers our social happenings: births, deaths, birthdays, illnesses of the most distinguished members of our society. And weddings as well! Gentlemen should be advised that, despite what her surname falsely suggests,

Señorita De León is still single and available. We
can assure you she is not one of those women who
go unnoticed.

It was a stupid job where the women of noble ancestry were
always *taking to their beds* and the gentlemen were always
returning from productive business trips, but it didn't matter:
Aurelia was inside the editorial office of a newspaper, among
typewriters and linotype machines; and that note was not mistaken: Aurelia de León did not go unnoticed. She liked that.
She liked that voices grew faint when she entered a room; she
liked that they looked at her from the far side over the heads
of many anonymous men, and that people crossed the room to
speak to her. One of those who did so, one of those who looked
at her from the far side and crossed the room, was a man of
forty-some years, in a bow tie, herringbone jacket, and clear-
framed glasses, who had just been in the paper—Aurelia had
seen his photo, and in which he'd been wearing the very same
jacket—for having published a novel about the Great War. My
father died in the war, was the first thing she said to him. Yes,
that's what I was told, he said. That's why I've come to speak
to you. Is that the only reason? she asked. Well, and also to
give you a copy of my book, he said, if you wouldn't take offense. And he added: But I don't happen to have one with me.
Well, then, she said, we're going to have to see each other

again, because I'm very curious about your book. The Colombian Remarque, the article said. What high praise, no? What an obligation, rather, he said. Because there is a tiny difference: Remarque fought in the war. I am almost ashamed to tell this to a daughter of a hero, but I don't even know how to fire a pistol. Please don't despise me.

Aurelia then found herself laying a delicate hand on the arm that held his drink, on the herringbone fabric that was much softer than she'd imagined, and telling him no, she didn't despise him at all.

They began to meet in downtown hotels, almost always at lunchtime, when they could both take leave of their worlds without awakening suspicions. His name was Pablo Durana; he had married fifteen years earlier, and from the first moment was painfully aware that he had married not for love, but to be able to do with his wife's money the only thing that interested him: read and write without any obligation to complicate his life. But they'd had three children because it was impossible not to have them, and thanks to them and due to them he had survived in that marriage the way others put up with a detestable but well-paid job, and in the meantime prepared the novel that would make him famous. Without haste, he said, but without rest.

All this he explained in long whispered sentences. Aurelia

de León, for her part, would have preferred not to know. She would in fact have preferred not to know anything about the man or his life, and if she could have begun again, she would have become his lover without even asking his name. The encounters with Pablo had been a discovery, that of another body and of her own body, and also the possibility of dispensing with uncomfortable suitors, even if she would do so for secret reasons the suitors would never find out.

With Pablo she could talk about books. While a Bogotá deluge lashed the windows and turned the Carrera Séptima into a river, Aurelia, naked on top of the covers, all the pores of her skin sealed against the cold, talked of Proust or Colette, and the following week Pablo would arrive with a cream-colored paperback he'd found on the new releases shelf—new releases a couple of years old by then—at the Librería Mundial. He was predictable, this man, and he was touching just by being predictable, but Aurelia wondered if she'd keep seeing him if she were able to go into the nearby cafés on her own, La Gran Vía, for example, to drink coffee with brandy and stand beside the piano and recite poetry until two in the morning without being taken for a bar girl and having men rub up against her as they passed between tables. And the answer was not clear. One thing was sure: if the guy didn't take her seriously, he pretended marvelously well that he did. At the same time, Aurelia could not forget that here, a hundred yards away, in the Café Automático or in the Windsor, things were happening, and Aurelia was not seeing them happen. In the cafés the journalists met with the poets; in the cafés the city was written. And Aurelia was not there. She could have told other stories, as she had told so many, and she wasn't telling them. But what did that matter?

One afternoon, after finishing writing up a page in which a young man left for Paris to study medicine and a lady called Jesusita passed over to a better life by the grace of our Lord, Aurelia rolled a blank piece of paper into the typewriter, wrote a letter to her own newspaper, and left it on her editor's desk. The letter appeared on the following Monday in a narrow column of *El Espectador*, beside an advertisement for overcoats and beneath a lament for the disappearance of the trees and flowers from the Plaza de Bolívar. Even though it had been shortened, even though it began with the ellipsis points of the amputation, Aurelia was satisfied.

> . . . All over the world women are fighting to get the right to vote; in Bogotá, gray and beautiful Bogotá, we'd be happy with the right to go into a café in the evenings. What secret world do these places hide that our chaste eyes cannot see? They say that the intellectual life of our city is carried on in those cafés; but perhaps a visitor from outside, who has a

clean view and clear judgment, will realize that
such life is, like the places where it is carried on,
nothing but smoke and mirrors . . .

That afternoon, the editor called her into his office. And
what was that? he asked. Aurelia looked at his black hair,
where the brilliantine was surviving in spite of it being past
four, and she noticed the plastic armband she'd never known
the name of. I want to write columns, she told him. I've been
working on trifles for a year and I'm tired of it. I have things
to say and I want to say them, not go on wasting time.

The editor looked at her over his thick-framed glasses. Au-
relita, he said, don't kid yourself: at your age, nobody has anything to say. But you go right ahead and find that out for
yourself. Write me something for tomorrow and I'll see what
I can do.

Aurelia wrote a column in a playful tone, with more irony
than sarcasm, that she titled "In Search of the Lost Woman."
She did not hand it to the editor, but waited for him to be away
from his desk to leave it there, and then she forgot about it,
buried as she was in her other obligations: the review of the
dance at El Venado, the first communion of a little girl with
long blond braids.

On the following Friday, when Pablo had already said
goodbye, she took a shower and got back under the covers,
waiting for her hair to dry while getting rid of some of the

exhaustion that had been with her since morning. And so, dressed and with her hair wrapped in a towel, she fell asleep. When she woke up, night had almost fallen. She was in a hurry, because they would already be setting the table at the Echavarrías' house, but instead of walking one street over to Séptima to catch the streetcar that would take her to her attic, she walked north without realizing it. The recent rain had left puddles beside the streetcar tracks, and Aurelia had to stay right up against the walls of the buildings to keep from being splashed by the passing cars. She turned the corner at Jiménez and walked toward the Sotomayor Building, and before she reached it could already hear the hubbub. It was like a smoked-glass display window, and inside everything was happening. She tried to enter, but a doorman held up the palm of his hand. Not allowed, he said. And as she tried to keep going, the guard added: There isn't even a ladies' room.

That doesn't matter, she answered. I've always peed standing up.

She went in as if making her way through the undergrowth. The smoke irritated her eyes; the smell of fried empanadas got up her nose. Then she heard a diaphanous voice imposing itself over the rest, as if he were giving a speech, and then she thought no, someone was reading poetry. And then she recognized her own words, read with proper intonation by a man to the small attentive audience of those around his bottle-covered table.

Where are these women? News reaches me here and there that talks about them as if they were unicorns. By way of example. I was told an anecdote that happened in the thermal baths of Paipa, where important people tend to summer. A recognized beauty arrived at the edge of the pool and took off the robe that covered her, revealing, to the scandal of those present, a black bikini like the ones in fashion on the beaches of Europe. The mayor immediately called one of his deputies and whispered something in his ear, after which he walked around to the other side of the pool, in full view of everyone, and when he found himself near the lady in question said to her, in a quite loud voice with the obvious intention of humiliating her:

"Señorita: our mayor would inform you that in this locality only one-piece swimsuits are permitted."

The young woman stood up, walked over to the edge of the pool, and from there, with her hands defiantly on her hips, shouted:

"Mr. Mayor, which one do you want me to take off?"

The guffaws reverberated around the narrow space of the Automático café. But before Aurelia could feel proud, before she could even think of approaching the group to bring herself to their attention, she felt in the pit of her stomach something that might have been pork lard. She didn't manage to reach the nonexistent ladies' room: after taking two steps she had to bend over and throw up beside a table, between the legs of clients who had been laughing at her witticisms, in the middle of a silence that in other circumstances would have struck her as magical.

Aurelia de León kept her pregnancy secret as long as possible. She didn't tell Pablo Durana anything, partly because she didn't want to cause him problems, partly because telling him would be chaining herself to him forever, or at least running that risk. She wanted to be alone; she did not require company. She did stop seeing Pablo: it was a curt breakup in two pitiless paragraphs, a model of warfare rhetoric that between men would have been reason enough for a duel. I know I am evasive, she wrote, I know I seem surly, but leave me alone.

She suffered her morning sickness in silence, left clandestine vomit in the Echavarrías' toilet, began to wear looser clothing so that later, when it was really necessary, nobody would notice a sudden change. For eight weeks she wrote her column, and readers celebrated it and welcomed a female voice on the opinion pages. Aurelia was careful not to get serious or solemn, because that would have annoyed her bosses: what they wanted, what the public wanted, was that sly tone. That's what they ordered: Go on, say it with that little tone of yours, everyone loves that. And she complied: no one had to twist her arm. The time would come to trouble them, but for now it was enough to enjoy what she had achieved. People talked about her latest column; other columnists quoted her once or twice; her colleagues in the newsroom invited her or tolerated her at their tables in the Automático, where there had only ever been one other woman: a writer named Matilde Castellanos, who had come from Nicaragua looking for a bullfighter she was in love with. She is a poetess, said the man who introduced them, and Matilde Castellanos corrected him: a poet, my friend, poet is just fine.

Then what had to happen did, what Aurelia expected would happen sooner or later. She returned to her attic one Thursday evening, after having heard León de Greiff read a handful of new poems, bringing the smell of cigar smoke into the house and, on her breath, the taste of brandy, and when she opened the door met the entire family. All the lights in the sitting room were on. Señor Echavarría received her with a question that was an accusation: And how long did you think you could hide a thing like this?

She said nothing: nothing she could have said would change anything, would turn back time, would avoid what was imminent. But what she didn't expect was the scorn in the voice of her friend, her classmate from school, veteran of the war against the nuns, the one responsible for Aurelia's having come to live in this house. We have been talking, Soledad said, and we all think you have to go have that baby somewhere else.

And then: We don't want any little whores here.

—————

Aurelia was almost four months pregnant when she returned to Nueva Lorena. She found a changed world. Everything was smaller: the coffee groves, the mill, the wooden bench where the pickers could sit and drink *aguapanela*. The farm administrator was a local man with a sharp voice and rolled-up trousers who had a name, Asdrúbal, but no surname, and who slept on the ground floor of the house with a woman too young to be the mother of his two grown daughters. Her grandmother Beatriz spent her days in a wicker rocking chair, blind for several years, which explained why her intermittent letters had ceased from one day to the next. Aurelia liked feeling the midday heat on her skin again; she enjoyed sleeping without wool socks, and getting out of bed at first light with a steaming cup of coffee in her hands, and breathing deeply on the second-floor balcony, without the air freezing her nostrils. It was another air, very different from the air in Bogotá, clearer, if you could say that, and carrying different scents. They were the smells of her childhood, the smell of the vegetation and manure and coffee, and she liked that. She also liked not having to give explanations and that there was nobody with enough authority to ask her for any. In this place, she thought, she could have her baby. It was like starting over, yes, like having a second opportunity. She had been right to come here, or the obligation to do so had been a stroke of luck.

She stopped writing columns, of course, but she didn't miss it: taking care of her grandmother, as well as her own pregnancy, took up all her hours, all her energy. During those months she lived apart from the outside world, ignorant of what was happening in the European war, oblivious of Hitler and Mussolini and the internecine struggles of Colombian politics, which reflected or reproduced the tensions of the war. She learned about coffee, about the new techniques, about the varieties that could be brought from elsewhere and that were more resistant to rust, about the correct way of planting bananas, which give shade and water to coffee. So, in her new world outside the world, the days and weeks and months flew by. She did not read the news of Rommel's arrival in Libya, or of Roosevelt's reelection, or the German invasion of the Soviet Union, nor did she know that the birth of her son roughly coincided with the decree ordering Jewish Germans to wear a yellow armband by way of identification. All this news came out in *El Espectador* and in *Semana* magazine, but nowhere, in no social section of any newspaper, did the news of the birth at Nueva Lorena of Gustavo Adolfo de León appear. Who wrote the society pages now, who had replaced Aurelia? She didn't even wonder about that.

Time passed.

Grandma Beatriz did not call one morning, as was her

custom, to be helped into the dining room; when Aurelia went to look for her, she found her fallen on the wooden floor, between the bed and the red door, with her nightdress around her hips. Aurelia thought how she had died without being able to see the child, her son's grandson, but most of all how she'd died before the child had learned to speak, and that, for some reason, seemed sadder. They buried her in the Cemetery of the Angels, beside her husband, on a sunny day when black clothing heated up and made sweat run down people's backs. The Mass in the church, on the steps that led to the village square, brought together more people than Aurelia had ever seen in that place. It was the first time she greeted Father Galindo, the parish priest, and she was surprised to find she was a head taller than he was. It was also the first time that people saw her, and saw her child and sometimes smiled at her, and saw the conspicuous absence of the father of that child. Gustavo Adolfo ran here and there, between the legs of the grown-ups, making little chirping sounds that would gradually come to resemble words. After the burial, Aurelia returned to the house at Nueva Lorena and found it enormous, and that night she slept thinking, stupidly, that her grandmother might come by to say farewell. Nobody ever slept in Beatriz's bed again, and only Asdrúbal's wife went in during the day, and only to dust, crossing herself and kissing the crucifix that hung round her neck.

Time passed.

———

The day Gustavo Adolfo turned six, news reached Nueva Lorena that a whole family, father, mother, and their three children, had been murdered on a village road south of Tolima, many miles away. They would not even have found out about it if Asdrúbal hadn't known the man, a swindler who had packed up all he had to try his luck somewhere else. They say things are getting ugly over there, Asdrúbal told her with his eyes fixed on the ground. Aurelia tried to calm him: over there was a very distant place, far from them and from Nueva Lorena and the village of Salento. She asked him to go into town and buy her a copy of *El Espectador*, and Asdrúbal returned with the only newspaper he could find in that small town in the afternoon: a copy of the previous day's *Diario del Quindío*, which the owner of the Colón Pharmacy gave him out of charity. And there, on eight pages of broadsheet, between a photo of a priest in a long cassock and ads for the Caldas chocolate shop and El Buen Gusto grocery store, Aurelia found out that yes, in fact, things were getting very ugly. There were stories about villages in Boyacá and in the Cauca Valley where bloodshed had sadly become an everyday occurrence; there were articles about traps someone had set during the last election; there was talk of assaults, stoning, and machete attacks. But this is not here, Aurelia said. Stay calm, Asdrúbal. All this is happening somewhere else.

Here there were other things to worry about: the hacienda, the coffee plants, the animals; a little boy with big eyes that weren't blue, but deeply black, like his father's. Gustavo Adolfo was almost the same age Aurelia was when she arrived for the first time at Nueva Lorena, hand in hand with a stranger who delivered her like a message from other strangers. Aurelia remembered those years of anarchy and told herself she could give her son the same happiness, and that here, far from the world, they would have a good life. The outside world was ugly; it was less ugly for a man as Gustavo Adolfo would be, but it was still ugly. Her task was to protect the child from the swipes the world's claws would take at him. What happened on a Sunday, in the early months of 1948, confirmed this.

The only version she heard was Asdrúbal's, but she had no reason to doubt its veracity. The man returned to the plantation one afternoon, after having gone to midday Mass, with a downcast expression on his face, and neither his wife nor his daughters stopped to greet Aurelia. Asdrúbal, wearing serge trousers and socks and shoes, took off his hat and told Aurelia that the priest had mentioned her in his sermon. Not directly, not by her proper name, but none of those present failed to recognize who he meant, because there was only one European woman who lived alone on a coffee plantation with a bastard son. Bastard? said Aurelia. That's what the priest said, Asdrúbal replied. And he also spoke of the deterioration of morals and good manners and how atheist liberalism is to blame for all of that, the poison that runs in the veins of our families, corrupting our children, who grow up without God or law. But bastard? Aurelia said. He said that? And Asdrúbal, looking at the hat he was crumpling in his hands, nodded.

In April, Gaitán was killed. Neither Asdrúbal nor his family had seen Aurelia cry the way she cried that day and the following days, beside the radio describing in alarmed voices what was happening in Bogotá. They hadn't even seen her cry when her grandmother Beatriz died; Aurelia noticed the bewilderment or accusation that covered their faces, but she couldn't explain. She was crying not just out of sadness, the sadness of having met that man—though only briefly: a photo session at a neighborhood hall—but out of other, new emotions that blended in her chest. The radio spat out threats and murderous slogans, calls for defense and revenge, daily discovered a new guilty party of the most horrendous crime in history. Aurelia listened with apprehension, the way you open the door to a room where you've heard a suspicious noise, but she turned down the volume if Gustavo Adolfo was near, because she had realized that the boy understood more than was apparent and his games had become nervous. Aurelia felt that it was her fault, though it wasn't: the outside world was to blame, the ugly world that invaded their world through the voice of the radio where deaths mounted and more were announced: liberals, conservatives, guerrillas, paramilitaries. All this was happening somewhere else, Aurelia told the boy, just as she'd told Asdrúbal earlier. But this time she knew she was lying, because it was soon clear that this time it wasn't, that in this country at war everything was happening everywhere, and it was only a matter of time until the war showed up in these parts. But Aurelia always believed that violence gave a warning, that it was like an animal whose heavy step can be heard from afar, and that she would know how to recognize the signs and escape in time.

The men arrived one January night, at dinnertime, as Aurelia and her son were helping themselves to a vegetable soup with a lot of noise of porcelain spoons, and chairs scraping against the floorboards. Neither Asdrúbal nor his family heard them approach, in spite of the dogs barking, and it was surely the barking that hid the sounds of the boots climbing the stairs. Later, when people from the village arrived to put the flames out, they found the dogs (or their charred and stiff bodies, their legs contracted as if threatening) still chained to the trees, as they were during the day, and regretted that Asdrúbal had not set them loose earlier that night. But they wouldn't have been able to do anything anyway, because the men came armed with machetes and rifles. They were not thieves or bandits, but a well-trained squad of what people were starting to call *pájaros*, and they had already left several dead in their journey up from the south. At the moment they arrived at the second floor, where the dining room was, and opened the door that was closed at night precisely so the dogs wouldn't come up, Gustavo Adolfo had left the table to go and better wash his hands, because his mother had examined them and found a trace of dirt under his nails. So the child heard the screams and struggles from the bathroom, and in the bathroom he kept silent in terror while the struggles and screams went on, and guessed that his mother was being dragged down the stairs and being asked who else was in the house, where the other person was. Gustavo Adolfo climbed up to the bathroom window, made himself small enough to fit through it, and jumped down to the balcony and the thud of his body landing on the boards scared him, but in a matter of seconds he was running down the back stairs, which led to the rooms of Asdrúbal and his family, and he found the doors open and the rooms empty and he had nobody to ask for help. Then he heard more screams, the screams of his mother suffering something unspeakable, and only knew to take off running, get into the coffee fields and run down the steep hill as fast as he could, but stepping sideways so he wouldn't fall flat on his face in the dirt. He ran down some two hundred yards, to the bottom of the small valley, and from there, with the skin of his arms and cheeks mercilessly scratched by the branches of the coffee shrubs, he looked up, toward where his house was, and he saw a new light illuminating the night, and then he saw that the light was fire, that his whole house was like a gigantic torch lit up against the night sky.

The people who came to put out the fire—the men of Salento, alerted by Asdrúbal—found the lifeless body of Aurelia de León. It was not charred like the bodies of the dogs, for the men, after raping her and slicing her throat, left her beside the crates where the beans are dried, and her body was hidden behind a brick-and-concrete wall that protected it from the flames. The Salento parish priest was very sorry not to be able to bury her in hallowed ground, beside her grandparents, for reasons that were, according to him, common knowledge; and Aurelia had nobody to defend her, or argue in her favor, or recount her life to establish the justice or injustice of that inter-diction. It meant nothing to Gustavo Adolfo, of course, that his mother was buried in a different cemetery, and he didn't remember even having noticed that the cemetery didn't have crosses or images of saints, for his mother had never talked to him of saints or explained the meaning of the cross.

As I have discovered, the Free Cemetery of Circasia was razed in the early 1950s, in the toughest years of the *Violencia*. The conservative armies, official or not, destroyed the statues pay-ing tribute to the founders, smashed up the gravestones and monuments with pickaxes, wrenched the iron gates from their hinges, dug up the anthuriums, and desecrated the tombs. Some human remains must have been moved to other places, but others were never recovered (the desecrations were painstaking and methodical in causing the greatest possible offense). The plaque I found on the monkey puzzle tree suggested, of course, that Aurelia de León's were among the lost remains. I don't know, I can never know, where those unhappy bones are now. Nor do I know who put up the plaque on the monkey puzzle tree, though I do know that the reconstruction of the cemetery took place in the 1970s when the war between the parties had ended, so the date on the plaque is thought-provoking: whoever put it up did so very soon after the cemetery was remade. I don't know who that person was, I say, but I can imagine: I imagine Gustavo Adolfo, the boy who saved his own life by hiding among the coffee bushes, growing up and becoming a man, and marrying very young to mitigate the solitude of being an orphan, or maybe never getting married, getting used to his solitude as his mother got used to hers, but with the advantage of being able to defend himself from undesired company with lines by León de Greiff, whom his mother knew before he'd written them:

I wish to be alone. I'll not be cured in company.
I want to taste silence, my sole incentive.

That's how I imagine him, yes, I like that image better: the image of a solitary man who one day, in his thirties, has a plaque made and puts it up in the cemetery where his mother was once buried. And maybe that leads him to remember her, to remember the life of his mother, and he realizes that he has begun to write a book.

Since I am Solitary,
Since I am Taciturn,
Leave me alone.

And he finishes it, telling in it all that he heard and remembered and had been able to find out in turn, just as I have found out so many things about him, and takes a verse that his mother would have liked, the same one he used for the plaque on the monkey puzzle tree, and uses it as an epigraph. And he publishes the book, perhaps at his own expense, and leaves it to rot in a printer's cellar because it only mattered that the book should exist, because this is the only consolation we have, the children of this inflamed country, condemned as we are to remember and investigate and lament, and then to compose songs for the flames.

DICCIONARIO ABREVIADO

DE

GALICISMOS, PROVINCIALISMOS Y CORRECCIONES

DE LENGUAJE

CON TRECIENTAS NOTAS EXPLICATIVAS

POR

RAFAEL URIBE U.

Primera edición

MEDELLIN
IMPRENTA DEL DEPARTAMENTO
1887

AUTHOR'S NOTE

Four of these stories have been published previously—sometimes in different versions—and I would like to express my gratitude to those publications and their editors. "El doble" ("The Double") appeared in the anthologies *Bogotá 39: Antología de cuento latinoamericano* (Ediciones B, Bogotá, 2007; edited by Guido Tamayo) and *Schiffe aus Feuer: 36 Geschichten aus Lateinamerika* (S. Fischer, Frankfurt, 2010; edited by Michi Strausfeld), and in the September 2017 issue of *Words Without Borders* (edited by Eric M. B. Becker). "Las malas noticias" ("Bad News") appeared in the anthology *El riesgo* (Rata_, Barcelona, 2017; edited by Ricard Ruiz Garzón). "Aeropuerto" ("Airport") appeared in the magazine *Aena Arte* (Madrid, 2008) and in *Les bonnes nouvelles de l'Amérique latine: Anthologie de la nouvelle latino-américaine contemporaine* (Gallimard, Paris, 2010; edited by Gustavo Guerrero and Fernando Iwasaki). A previous version of "El último corrido" ("The Last

Corrido") appeared in the anthologies *Calibre 39* (Villegas Editores, Bogotá, 2007; edited by Luis Fernando Charry) and *The Future Is Not Ours* (Open Letter, University of Rochester, 2012; edited by Diego Trelles Paz; translation by Janet Hendrickson).

My gratitude, as always, goes to this book's first readers, who made it better with their comments, suggestions, and good judgment: Pilar Reyes, María Lynch, Carolina Reoyo, and Adriana Martínez. And to Mariana, who not only read these stories before anyone else, but was often responsible for their occurring to me.

J.G.V.

Bogotá, September 2018